A missing child

Amy stared at the cat, wondering how it had gotten there.

If Kendra had climbed out of bed by herself and had gone exploring, the cat would still be with her. Amy knew that as surely as she knew her own name. If Kendra had dropped the little cat, she would have picked it up. She would not willingly have left Tubby behind.

But if someone was carrying Kendra, and Tubby slipped from her hand, that person might not stop to retrieve the toy. That person might be in a hurry.

Shivers ran up Amy's arms. She picked up the little cat and carried it back to the house.

She knew.

She would have given anything to make the knowledge go away, but she couldn't. It was there, coiled inside her. It pressed all around her, a heavy dread hanging in the air, pushing down on Amy, ready to smother her with each breath she took.

She knew.

Kendra had been kidnapped.

ALSO BY

PEG KEHRET

Abduction!

Cages

Danger at the Fair

Don't Tell Anyone

Earthquake Terror

The Ghost's Grave

Horror at the Haunted House

I'm Not Who You Think I Am

Nightmare Mountain

Searching for Candlestick Park

Spy Cat

The Stranger Next Door

Terror at the Zoo

PEG KEHRET

Stolen Children

PUFFIN BOOKS
An Imprint of Penguin Group (USA) Inc.

PUFFIN BOOKS
Published by the Penguin Group
Penguin Young Readers Group, 345 Hudson Street, New York, New York 10014, U.S.A.
Penguin Group (Canada), 90 Eglinton Avenue East, Suite 700, Toronto, Ontario, Canada M4P 2Y3
(a division of Pearson Penguin Canada Inc.)
Penguin Books Ltd, 80 Strand, London WC2R 0RL, England
Penguin Ireland, 25 St Stephen's Green, Dublin 2, Ireland (a division of Penguin Books Ltd)
Penguin Group (Australia), 250 Camberwell Road, Camberwell, Victoria 3124, Australia
(a division of Pearson Australia Group Pty Ltd)
Penguin Books India Pvt Ltd, 11 Community Centre, Panchsheel Park, New Delhi - 110 017, India
Penguin Group (NZ), 67 Apollo Drive, Rosedale, North Shore 0632, New Zealand
(a division of Pearson New Zealand Ltd.)
Penguin Books (South Africa) (Pty) Ltd, 24 Sturdee Avenue,
Rosebank, Johannesburg 2196, South Africa

Registered Offices: Penguin Books Ltd, 80 Strand, London WC2R 0RL, England

First published in the United States of America by Dutton Children's Books,
a division of Penguin Young Readers Group, 2008
Published by Puffin Books, a division of Penguin Young Readers Group, 2010

11 13 15 17 19 20 18 16 14 12

LIBRARY OF CONGRESS CATALOGING-IN-PUBLICATION DATA
Kehret, Peg.
Stolen children / Peg Kehret.
p. cm.
Summary: Fourteen-year-old Amy's excitement over her first babysitting job ends when she and her three-year-old charge are kidnapped, but a daily videorecording sent to little Kendra's parents allows Amy to send clues, in hopes of being rescued before the kidnappers decide they no longer need her.
ISBN 978-0-14-241513-9 (pbk.)
[1. Kidnapping—Fiction. 2. Babysitters—Fiction. 3. Signals and signaling—Fiction.] I. Title.
PZ7.K2518Sso 2010
[Fic]—dc22
2009015412

Puffin Books ISBN 978-0-14-241513-9

Designed by Irene Vandervoort
Set in Perpetua

Printed in the United States of America

A few reasons why this book is dedicated to Myra and Larry Karp:

Visits

Chocolate cake

Literary discussions

Memories of Carl

Knitting lessons

Peg piles

More visits

Cinnamon rolls

Schwartz's author photo

Pizza

Book loans

Medical consultations

Still more visits

Sage advice

No-reason surprise presents

Sharing the epistles

Political discussions

Liking my vegetarian meals

Understanding Lucy

Mariners baseball

Honest opinions

Calendar dates

And, most of all, the visits—

which entertain, energize, and enlighten me.

Acknowledgments

Thanks to Detective Robert Onishi of the Renton, Washington, Police Department for reading this manuscript and helping me describe the police procedures accurately; to Clarice Martin for putting me in touch with Detective Onishi; to Casey Karp for providing up-to-date information about camcorders and for cheerfully bailing me out whenever I have a computer problem; to Anne Konen for checking the Caravan facts and for prompt and efficient proofreading; to Merrie Lou Daggett for keeping my post office box stuffed with fan mail; to Emilie Jacobson, my agent at Curtis Brown, Ltd., for sending me money; to Anna Abreu for her efficiency while Emilie recovered from an auto accident; and to the fantastic group at Dutton Children's Books for their expertise and enthusiasm.

Stolen Children

DAY ONE

Chapter One

Amy's babysitting course taught her basic first aid, bedtime tips, and how to change a diaper, but it did not cover what to do if two thugs with a gun showed up. She had to figure that out by herself.

The trouble started with a phone call, on a Monday late in June.

"Is this Amy Nordlund?" a woman asked.

"Yes."

"This is Elyse Edgerton. I got your name from Mrs. Montag at the community center. She said you've completed the babysitting class."

"That's right." The name meant nothing to Amy. Later she would learn that the Edgerton family owned a tugboat company, a custom sailboat company, and many acres of prime waterfront property, including the Raven building—a high-rise of luxury apartments overlooking Puget Sound, with upscale boutiques on the ground level. They also owned a resort hotel in Hawaii.

"Mrs. Montag told me you are fourteen," Mrs. Edgerton said. "Is that correct?"

"Yes."

"I don't usually hire anyone that young, but I'm in a bit of a bind. My mother just fell and broke her leg; I need to go to the hospital, and I don't have anyone to watch my daughter, Kendra.

I don't want to take a three-year-old with me to the emergency room. Could you come right now, and stay for about four hours? I can pick you up."

"I need to call my mom first, to be sure it's okay."

"While you do that, do you have any references I can check?"

Amy gave the names of the only two people who had hired her so far. Mrs. Edgerton said she'd call back after she had talked with them.

Amy's mom was in a meeting, so Amy called Mrs. Montag to be sure she had given Amy's name to Mrs. Edgerton.

"Oh, yes, dear," Mrs. Montag said. "I hope you can help her out. You're lucky to get such a job."

When Mrs. Edgerton called back, Amy said she could come. She left a message on her mom's voice mail, giving Mrs. Edgerton's phone number. She changed into clean jeans, combed her hair, and put a monkey hand puppet into her purse. Ten minutes later, a silver sedan pulled up in front of her house, and Amy ran out to meet her new employer.

Mrs. Edgerton was pleasant, elegant, and clearly worried about her mother. Kendra, a dimpled toddler in yellow overalls, was strapped into a car seat in the backseat.

"Hi, Kendra," Amy said.

The little girl gave her a drooly grin and continued to play with a grubby-looking stuffed cat.

"I like your cat," Amy said. "What's your cat's name?"

"Tubby," Kendra said. "This be Tubby."

"Hi, Tubby," Amy said.

"I'm sorry this is such short notice," Mrs. Edgerton said. "Usually my nanny would be with Kendra but Darielle got invited on an impromptu trip, so I gave her this week off, and I took vacation time. Kendra's had lunch and it's almost time for her nap.

Her schedule is posted on the fridge; I keep that up-to-date. There's a list of any phone numbers you might need, including my cell phone. My husband's out of town, so I'm the only contact today, but I'm sure you won't need anything."

She glanced in the rearview mirror. "Kendra's a sweetheart. She won't give you any grief."

The car pulled into a circular driveway and stopped before an impressive brick house. While Amy admired the manicured lawn and lush flower beds, Mrs. Edgerton took Kendra out of her car seat.

As soon as they were inside, Mrs. Edgerton said, "I hate to just dump you like this, but I have to rush. Be a good girl, Kendra. Amy's going to play with you and give you some ice cream." She gave her daughter a quick hug, thanked Amy for being there, and promised to be home by six o'clock. A trace of expensive perfume lingered in the air after she left.

"Ice cweam?" Kendra said, heading toward the kitchen.

"Sounds good to me," Amy said. She opened the freezer compartment above the refrigerator and saw six pints of Ben & Jerry's finest. Amy's mom bought the store brands on sale; Amy liked this job already.

"What kind do you want?" she asked. "Vanilla? Strawberry?"

"Choca Chip Cookie Dough," said Kendra. "Tubby want Choca Chip Cookie Dough."

Amy found bowls and spoons, and sat down to enjoy the treat. While they ate, Kendra pretended to feed ice cream to the toy cat, and Amy read through the instructions that were on the fridge. No surprises there.

After they ate the ice cream, Amy took Kendra to her bedroom for her nap, making sure Kendra used the bathroom first, as directed.

"Blankee," said Kendra, reaching for a faded blue blanket that was folded at the foot of the bed.

Amy covered her with the blue blanket, then read two stories aloud.

"Tubby go night-night," Kendra said as she made sure her stuffed cat was also under the blanket. Then she stuck her thumb in her mouth, closed her eyes, and quickly fell asleep. What an angel, Amy thought. Mrs. Montag was right; Amy was lucky to have this assignment. Maybe if she did a really good job, she'd be asked to come again.

Amy desperately wanted to show that she was trustworthy. Even though it was too late to prove it to her dad, she needed to prove it to herself.

As always, thinking about her dad brought tears to Amy's eyes. She wanted to forget that horrible conversation with him, but no matter how hard she tried to ignore the memory, it stayed with her. Whenever she thought about it, she felt shriveled, like an orange left too long in the fridge.

Why hadn't she admitted her error, and apologized? Why had she been so stubborn and defensive? Most of all, why hadn't she told Dad and Mom what had happened right away, instead of staying silent and hoping they wouldn't find out?

The problem had been completely her fault. She had agreed to feed the next-door neighbor's golden retriever, Lucky, and take him for a walk because Mr. Prendell, who lived alone, had to go straight from work to a meeting that night and wouldn't be home until midnight.

Amy had taken care of Lucky many times before. She knew where Mr. Prendell hid a house key, and where Lucky's food and leash were kept. Whenever Mr. Prendell couldn't get home on time, he called Amy, and she fed and exercised Lucky. Usually

Amy stayed a while and played with Lucky or brushed him. She couldn't have a pet of her own because her mom was allergic to animal fur, so it was a treat for Amy to visit Lucky, and Mr. Prendell always left five dollars on the counter for her.

That last time, Mr. Prendell had called on a Tuesday evening, and asked Amy to come on Wednesday. She had agreed.

He called again on Thursday. "What happened last night?" he asked. "Your money was still here and Lucky acted hungry when I got home."

As soon as she heard his voice, Amy realized what she had done. "Oh!" she said. "Oh, Mr. Prendell, I completely forgot! I'm sorry! Was Lucky okay?"

"It didn't hurt him to wait for his dinner, but there was a big wet spot on the carpet next to the back door."

Amy felt sick. "I had planned to come as soon as I got home from gymnastics," she said, "but my aunt and uncle from Texas stopped in unexpectedly. They were in town on a business trip and decided to surprise us, and then we all went out for dinner, and when we got back, my dad showed some home videos and I simply forgot about Lucky. I am so sorry!" She closed her eyes, not wanting to think about Lucky waiting by the door to be let out.

Mr. Prendell was nice about it, but Amy felt terrible. How could she have done such a thing? Poor Lucky! Next time Mr. Prendell asked her to dog-sit, she would write herself a note. If there ever was a next time. Amy wouldn't blame Mr. Prendell if he found someone else to take care of Lucky.

She knew she should tell her parents what had happened, but she was ashamed that she'd forgotten Lucky, and she didn't want anyone to know, so she said nothing to them. That turned out to be an even bigger mistake than forgetting to take care of Lucky, because Mr. Prendell happened to see Amy's dad out by the mailboxes a few days later.

Mr. Nordlund had been leaving for work, but he stormed back inside to confront Amy. "I just talked to Tim Prendell," he said. "I understand you let him and Lucky down."

It was one of those days when Amy felt as if she couldn't do anything right. Twenty minutes earlier, Mom had snapped at her because Amy had neglected to unload the dishwasher the night before. Amy had meant to, but she had a report due, and by the time she finished her homework, she forgot about the dishwasher.

That morning, Mom was rushing around, getting ready for work, and when she opened the dishwasher to put in her cereal bowl and found it full of clean dishes, she acted as if it were a federal crime to forget a chore.

Amy already felt incpt that morning, and it was only seven o'clock. Now her dad stood beside her, looking furious. Amy stared silently at her toast.

"Why didn't you tell us what had happened?" he asked. "We would have offered to have Mr. Prendell's carpet cleaned."

It had not occurred to her that her parents could help make up for her blunder.

"I can't believe you were so irresponsible," her dad went on. "When you say you will pet-sit, you are agreeing to care for a living creature. Lucky is Mr. Prendell's best friend! He trusts you to be sure Lucky is fed and comfortable. Instead, you let Lucky go hungry and made him wait to go to the bathroom until he couldn't hold it any longer and had to wet on the rug, which he knew he shouldn't do."

"I told Mr. Prendell I was sorry," Amy said.

"I would hope so! But saying you're sorry is not enough. You should have offered to take Lucky for a walk every day for a month, or told Mr. Prendell that the next five pet-sitting jobs were free. You can't just be sorry for your mistakes; you have to take action to make amends. What if Mr. Prendell had been gone overnight, as he sometimes is?"

Amy knew her dad was right, but she was afraid if she admitted it, she'd burst into tears and end up going to school with red eyes and blotchy skin. So instead of acknowledging her error and apologizing, she mumbled, "Everybody makes mistakes. You aren't perfect."

"No, I'm not," he said. "But when I say I'll do something, I keep my word. I'm ashamed of you."

He turned then, went out to his car, and drove off.

Three hours later, in the middle of a spelling test, Amy was called to the principal's office. Wondering what else she had done wrong, Amy entered the office.

Her mom waited for her there. Amy could tell from the look on her mom's face that something bad had happened.

"Your dad had an accident on his way to work," Mom said, her voice choked with tears. "A speeding driver ran a red light, hit Dad's car broadside, and—and killed him."

Just like that, her dad was gone.

Chapter Two

Amy felt as if she'd been turned to ice. She would crack into a thousand pieces if she tried to move.

Her mom, sobbing now, put her arms around Amy and hugged her hard, but Amy did not respond. In that first, horrible moment of understanding what Mom was telling her, Amy remembered her dad's last words to her, hearing his voice as clearly as if he stood beside her. "I'm ashamed of you."

In the three months since then, Amy had relived that final morning in her mind a thousand times, wishing she could take it back and do it over.

The last thing she had said to him was, "You aren't perfect."

Maybe he wasn't perfect—who is?—but he was a great dad who played Scrabble with her, and built her a balance beam so she could practice her gymnastics routine. He actually read the books she liked, and then discussed them with her. He took her and Jorja, her best friend, ice-skating every winter, and he came to all her school events, and watched baseball games on TV with her.

If Amy could live that morning over again, she would say, "You're right. I'm sorry, Dad. I love you."

Even more terrible than those hurtful last words was knowing that if he had not come back to talk to her about Lucky, he would have left for work five or six minutes earlier. He would have been safely through the intersection before the speeding driver got there.

No one ever blamed Amy for the accident because nobody else knew that her dad had returned to talk to her that morning. But Amy knew.

She kept her terrible secret: her dad's death was her fault and no matter how much she regretted her behavior, nothing would ever bring him back.

Amy pushed the memory of that morning away, and wandered through the Edgertons' house, which looked as if it should be featured in *House Beautiful* or *Today's Interior Design*. It wasn't formal, though. Kendra's toys were scattered about, and the books stacked on the coffee table looked as if they were there to be read, not just to serve as part of the decor.

A sliding door led from the kitchen/family room to a large patio and an adjoining swimming pool. Amy went out, leaving the door open a foot so she could hear Kendra if she woke up and called to her. She stretched out on a lounge chair, and thought how great it would be to live in a house like this. Not that it was likely to ever happen.

Amy and her mom had a cozy two-bedroom house with nice neighbors, but the whole thing would fit in the Edgertons' kitchen. Amy's parents had hoped to buy a larger house in a year or so, but that plan had died along with Amy's dad.

Amy didn't mind staying in their old house. It was comforting to be in familiar surroundings, where she had so many memories of her dad. Her mom didn't want to move now, either.

"I've had too much change in my life," Mom said. "I wouldn't buy a different house now, even if I could afford to."

Neither of them said it, but they now had less need of extra space, since only two people lived there instead of three.

Without Dad's salary, money was tight. Amy hoped to earn enough this summer to pay for her own clothes and maybe even help a little with groceries. Probably not Ben & Jerry's, but she could buy the peanut butter and apples and bagels that were mainstays of her diet.

Dad had told her it wasn't enough to be sorry for a mistake; she needed to take action to atone. She now walked Lucky every day, at no charge. She had taken the babysitting course, and she was earning some money to show that she was responsible.

Amy made a mental note to call the community center tomorrow, to thank Mrs. Montag for recommending her to Mrs. Edgerton.

Feeling relaxed in the sun, Amy closed her eyes. She thought about "Winning Secrets," a story she was writing. For as long as she could remember, Amy had wanted to be a writer, and she had several notebooks and computer files of original stories and poems. She thought "Winning Secrets" was her best effort yet, especially the parts where her characters used a secret signal to communicate.

Amy jumped at a sudden noise. Was Kendra awake?

Amy looked at her watch. Three o'clock. She must have dozed off, because she had put Kendra to bed at one-thirty. Mrs. Edgerton had said Kendra usually slept about two hours.

Amy hurried inside to check on the little girl. As she started upstairs, she heard what sounded like a car engine.

Was Mrs. Edgerton home already? Had someone come to the door while she was out by the pool? Had the doorbell rung, or had someone knocked? Perhaps that's what woke her. Maybe a package had been delivered. She went to the front door and opened it. There was no package, nothing to indicate that anyone had been there.

Amy closed the door, climbed the stairs, and went into Kendra's room.

The bed was empty.

"Kendra?" Amy said. "Where are you?"

Was she hiding? Playing a game?

"Kendra!" Amy called. "Let's have some more ice cream."

Her voice echoed in the empty room. Her heart hammered in her chest. *Where was Kendra?*

Amy looked in the bathroom. She ran from room to room, calling, looking under beds, yanking open closet doors. Fear ran with her, making her hands shake.

"Kendra!" Amy shouted. "Kendra, answer me!"

She remembered the swimming pool. A fence guarded against accidents; could the gate have been unlocked? Oh, please, no, she thought as she rushed back downstairs. If Kendra had tumbled into the pool, the splash would have awakened me. Wouldn't it? I was sitting right there, next to the water. Surely I would have heard her.

Amy raced through the family room and out to the patio, her eyes scanning the smooth surface of the water as she approached the pool. Only a white safety ring floated on the clear blue water. She ran to the edge of the pool, where wide steps invited swimmers to enter.

Her eyes darted from one side of the pool to the other. Kendra wasn't there.

Her relief that Kendra had not drowned was quickly replaced by dread. Had Kendra let herself out the door? Had she wandered off through the neighborhood? Gone into the street? Awful possibilities, each worse than the last, flashed through Amy's mind like a slide show.

Remembering the car's engine that she had heard, she wondered who had been here. What had they done?

She returned to the house, ran to the front door, and opened it again. This time she hurried down the curved path toward the circular driveway. Had someone come in the house while she slept and taken Kendra? Who?

Kendra's father was out of town. Her grandmother was in the hospital. Her nanny was on vacation. Nobody else was on the list of personal phone numbers. There was no one with a legitimate reason to come in the Edgertons' home.

Amy thought back, trying to remember if the front door had been locked. She remembered Mrs. Edgerton hugging Kendra when they arrived at the house, telling her daughter to be good, rushing away. She had not pushed the door lock before she went out, and Amy had not locked it after she left.

Why didn't I lock the door? WHY?

She had learned in her babysitting class to always keep the doors locked when she was babysitting. After Mrs. Edgerton left, she could easily have turned the lock, but she hadn't even thought of it. She had been too eager to give Kendra her ice cream, to establish a connection so the child would like her.

Amy looked around the yard, listening, hoping she might still hear a little girl say, "Ice cweam," and see her running toward home. She heard only the drone of a small airplane, high overhead.

As Amy turned to go back to the house, something caught her eye—a small striped lump lying at the base of one of the shrubs that edged the path. She looked closer. Tubby.

Kendra's stuffed toy, the grungy cat that she had played with in the car, and had pretended to feed, and had clutched as she fell asleep, lay in the dirt.

Amy stared at the cat, wondering how it had gotten there.

If Kendra had climbed out of bed by herself and had gone exploring, the cat would still be with her. Amy knew that as surely as she knew her own name. If Kendra had dropped the little cat, she would have picked it up. She would not willingly have left Tubby behind.

But if someone was carrying Kendra, and Tubby slipped from her hand, that person might not stop to retrieve the toy. That person might be in a hurry.

Shivers ran up Amy's arms and for a minute she feared the ice cream was going to reappear. She picked up the little cat and carried it back to the house.

She knew.

She would have given anything to make the knowledge go away, but she couldn't. It was there, coiled inside her. It pressed all around her, a heavy dread hanging in the air, pushing down on Amy, ready to smother her with each breath she took.

She knew.

Kendra had been kidnapped.

Chapter Three

Amy wondered if she should call the police first, or call Mrs. Edgerton and let her call the police. In the second that she hesitated, trying to decide, she heard a vehicle roar into the Edgertons' driveway.

Hoping it would be Mrs. Edgerton, Amy rushed to the front door again. Even if it was the mail truck or FedEx or the gardener, at least it would be an adult. Right then, Amy felt as if she needed a grown-up at her side. Even though she dreaded telling Mrs. Edgerton that Kendra was missing, Amy couldn't cope with this on her own.

She flung open the door and rushed out just as a tall man leaped from a van and ran toward her, leaving the door open.

Amy hurried toward him. "I need help," she said.

The man looked at her as if she had three heads, as if he could not believe what he was seeing.

Amy heard Kendra before she saw her.

"Tubby!" Kendra sobbed. "Me want Tubby!"

Amy froze, staring at the man. Behind him, through the windshield, she saw Kendra in the car.

Amy whirled around and dashed back toward the house.

A deep voice from the car shouted, "Stop her!"

Footsteps slapped the path behind her.

Amy raced inside, slammed the door, and locked it. Then she ran to the kitchen, looking for a phone. She saw the base of a portable phone on the small desk next to the oven, but the receiver wasn't there. Mrs. Edgerton must have used it, then set it down somewhere.

As Amy searched frantically around the room, she heard the front door open. She had just locked it; the man had a key to the Edgertons' house!

This didn't make sense. Even if he had a right to be here, he shouldn't take Kendra.

She finally spotted the phone on the counter, by the toaster. She grabbed it, punched *talk*, got a dial tone, jabbed *nine*.

She had not yet hit the *one, one* when the tall man burst into the room. He held a small black gun, pointed at her.

"Drop the phone," he said. "Now."

Amy laid the phone on the counter. She noticed a wrinkled sheet of notebook paper near the sink. It had not been there earlier, when she rinsed the ice-cream dishes.

In an instant, the man reached Amy. He snatched the phone, listened for a second, tapped *off*, and then put it down again.

A second man strode into the kitchen. He was older, with long strands of hair combed carefully over his balding head. "Smokey!" he said. "You promised no guns."

"She was trying to call for help," the tall one said.

"Did the call go through?"

"No. I got here in time." Smokey looked at Amy as he talked, but his eyes seemed to see straight through her, as if she weren't really there. Several days' growth of beard sprouted on his face, and his uneven hair looked greasy, as if he had not shampooed it for many days. He put the gun in his pocket. "Let's get out of here," he said.

"What are we going to do about this girl?" the older man asked.

Both men glared at Amy as if she had caused the problem.

"She'll have to come with us," Smokey said.

"Kidnap *both* of them?"

"We can't leave her here; she'd have the cops after us before we could start the engine." He looked at Amy and jerked his head toward the front door, as if telling her to go that way.

She stayed where she was.

The older man walked toward the front door.

Smokey grabbed Amy's wrists and held them behind her, forcing her to walk in front of him. He pushed her through the house. When they reached the door, Amy saw Tubby on the floor, where she had dropped him when she turned the lock.

"There's her toy," Amy said. "That's what she's crying for."

"Hugh," Smokey said. "Pick up the toy. She's going to attract the attention of half the county if she doesn't get it."

Hugh stuffed the cat in his pocket. "Spoiled brat," he muttered.

As soon as they went outside, Amy looked toward the van. She hoped Kendra had climbed out to look for Tubby while the men were inside the house, but the tear-streaked face peered from the window and Amy heard a loud wail, "Tub-by!" followed by a hiccup.

"Open the door, Kendra!" Amy shouted. "Get out of the car and run!"

"Smokey!" Hugh glared at the man behind Amy. "Keep her quiet!"

"Help!" Amy yelled.

Keeping one hand on Amy's wrists, Smokey clamped the other hand over her mouth. "One more sound," he muttered, "and I use the gun."

As Hugh sprinted to the car, the back door opened, and Kendra slid out. Hurry, Kendra, Amy thought. Run! Go to a neighbor's house and tell them what happened.

Instead, Kendra stood beside the car, watching the two men and Amy hurry toward her. "Tubby?" she asked.

Hugh reached Kendra, picked her up, and set her back in the car.

Seconds later, Smokey shoved Amy into the backseat with Kendra.

Amy didn't try to get away. Even if she could have freed herself from the man's strong hands, she didn't want to escape without Kendra.

Amy patted the child's shoulder. "It will be okay," she said. "I'm going with you. I'll take care of you."

Even though Amy was more scared than she had ever been in her life, she tried to appear confident so that Kendra wouldn't be frightened. No matter what happened, she would watch out for Kendra. She was responsible for this little girl, and she would do whatever was necessary to keep her safe.

Smokey got behind the wheel and started the engine.

Amy took a tissue out of her jeans pocket and wiped Kendra's nose.

Hugh sat turned sideways, with one arm on the back of his seat. He looked at Amy. "Don't even think about yelling for help," he said.

"We were easy on you just now," Smokey said, "because we didn't want to hang around here any longer than we have to, but if you do anything to attract attention, you'll wish you hadn't. And so will the kid."

"Tubby fall!" Kendra said, her voice quivering. "Tubby in mud."

"She wants her toy," Amy said.

Hugh fished the cat out of his pocket and tossed it over his shoulder. It landed on the floor in front of Kendra. Amy retrieved it and gave it to Kendra.

"She needs a car seat," Amy said. "She's too little to ride without a car seat."

"Tough," Smokey said.

"It's not legal for her to ride without a car seat," Amy said. "If a police officer sees her riding this way, you'll get pulled over."

Smokey shrugged, indicating he couldn't care less, but Hugh glanced quickly in all directions, as if looking for a patrol car. He's nervous, Amy thought. He's afraid of getting stopped by the police.

"Sit here, Kendra," Amy said, patting the center of the backseat. "You get to wear a seat belt today, just like the big kids do."

As Amy buckled her own seat belt, Kendra wriggled over until she was sitting where Amy had indicated, then let Amy pull the center seat belt around her and buckle it. It wasn't as good as a car seat, but it was better than no protection at all.

"Where are we going?" Amy asked.

"You're gonna be a movie star," Smokey said. "You're gonna be filmed by the great videographer, the one and only Smokey Sanderson."

"I never should have agreed to do this," Hugh said. "If you weren't my nephew, I would never have said I'd do it."

"You don't want to be rich?" Smokey asked. "You don't want to split half a million in cold cash? 'Cause if you don't, you can drop out right now, and I'll take your share."

"Keeping a three-year-old for a week was one thing. This is a whole other deal." Hugh glanced at Amy.

A week! Amy thought. They're going to keep us for a whole week?

"Nothing's changed," Smokey said, "except now two families will be desperate to get their kid back, instead of only one. Every day's video will be that much more important. Old Smokey's gonna make those dudes so eager to get their kids that they'll be begging us to take their cash!"

Hugh turned to look at Amy. "Why were you at the Edgerton house?" he asked. "Darielle was supposed to be the only one there."

"I was babysitting. I'm taking care of Kendra."

"Babysitting!" Hugh glared at Smokey. "What happened to Darielle? I thought your girlfriend was the nanny."

"She was."

"Was? Are you saying she isn't anymore? This whole deal was based on having Darielle there as our inside contact."

"I think she's still the nanny," Smokey said.

"You think? Don't you know? What's going on that you haven't told me?"

"Nothing, Hugh. Nothing! It's just that Darielle and me, well, we split last week."

"You split."

"Yeah. She needs some time by herself."

"She dumped you."

"No! She just—"

"She dumped you and you didn't tell me, and we went ahead with your scheme even though your ex-girlfriend knows all about it. What if she tells the cops?"

"Relax. You worry too much. She won't tell because if she does, she won't get the fifty thousand bucks that I promised her for letting me copy the front-door key and for telling me the mother's work schedule so I'd come when Darielle would be the only one there."

"But she wasn't there. This girl was taking care of the kid." He looked at Amy again. "Why were you babysitting?" he asked. "Where was the nanny?"

"She's on vacation," Amy said. "She went on a trip."

Hugh groaned.

"She did?" said Smokey.

"What if the Edgertons post a big reward for information that leads to Kendra's safe return?" Hugh said. "What if they offer a hundred thousand dollars?"

"Darielle still won't tell," said Smokey.

"Right. Her deep love for the loser she broke up with will keep her lips sealed, and she'll pass up a huge reward."

"She can't tell because she was in on it."

Hugh nodded. "You're right. By giving you the key and the mother's work schedule, Darielle became an accomplice. If she turns you in, she gets herself in trouble."

"Besides, she knows that if she tells, I'll kill her."

Smokey said it as casually as if he were saying, "She knows I'll call her."

The words hung in the air.

He means it, Amy thought.

A chill crept down the back of her neck. She and Kendra had been kidnapped by a man who was capable of murder.

Chapter Four

Elyse Edgerton left her mother's hospital room reluctantly. She wished she could remain through the evening, to make sure her mom was comfortable and to be there when the doctor made his evening rounds.

But she had promised Amy she'd be home by six, and even though the girl was highly recommended and seemed capable, she had never stayed with Kendra before. Mrs. Edgerton wanted to be home in time to give Kendra her dinner and bath.

She dialed her home number on her cell phone as she walked across the hospital parking garage to her car, intending to let Amy know she was on her way. It rang five times, and then the voice-mail service picked up the call. Mrs. Edgerton hung up. Amy and Kendra must be outside, she thought. Maybe they're playing ball or Kendra's digging in the sandbox.

As she drove home, she made plans for the next day. If everything had gone well today, and Kendra seemed happy with her new sitter, Mrs. Edgerton would see if Amy could babysit again tomorrow.

The garage opened directly into the family room. The sliding door stood open, so Mrs. Edgerton walked out to the patio. She glanced at the sandbox. Kendra's yellow bucket and shovel were planted in the sand, but she didn't see Kendra.

"Hello!" she called. "I'm home."

There was no answer.

Mrs. Edgerton frowned. Why had Amy left the sliding door

open, if she wasn't close by? Mrs. Edgerton walked past the pool and looked toward Kendra's swing set. "Hello!" she called again. "Where's my girl?"

Usually when Mrs. Edgerton arrived home, Kendra came running from wherever she had been playing, shouting, "Mommy! Mommy!" She always wrapped her arms around her mother's legs, and insisted that her mother give Tubby a hello kiss. Now the house was quiet. Too quiet.

Mrs. Edgerton went back inside and up the stairs to Kendra's room. Her daughter's favorite blanket was in a heap on the bed, so she had taken a nap.

Maybe they went for a walk, Mrs. Edgerton thought. Maybe Amy had taken Kendra around the block. But surely she would not have left the house without locking the doors. That open sliding door did not seem right.

A lump of dread formed in Mrs. Edgerton's throat as she went back downstairs and into the family room. This time her eyes swept across the countertops, and she saw a piece of notebook paper lying beside the sink.

Oh, thank goodness. Amy had left a note. Letting out her breath in relief, she reached for the paper.

The handwriting was messy; the paper itself looked as if it had been crumpled, thrown away, and then retrieved.

We have your daughter. You'll get a video to prove she's okay. DO NOT CALL POLICE. Do nothing until the video arrives. It will contain your instructions.

Mrs. Edgerton's hands shook so hard the paper rattled. She leaned against the counter to steady herself.

Someone had kidnapped her child.

She dialed her husband's cell phone. By the time he answered, she was crying so hard she could hardly talk. "Kendra's gone," she sobbed. "Somebody stole Kendra."

"How?" he said. "What happened?"

Mrs. Edgerton took a deep breath, and then told him everything, starting with her mom breaking her leg.

"So where is the new sitter?"

"I don't know. She isn't here. Maybe the kidnappers took her, too."

"Or maybe she was in on the plot."

"I don't think so. She's young, and Mrs. Montag recommended her as the best student in the babysitting class. Oh, Kurt, what are we going to do?"

"We'll start by calling the police."

"The note says not to. That part is in capital letters."

"I don't care if it's painted in gold. We have to call the police. We can't deal with this by ourselves."

"The kidnapper might hurt Kendra. If we don't do what he says, we might not get her back."

"We can't sit around and wait for a video to be delivered. That could take a couple of days, and meanwhile we don't know where our daughter is or what's happening to her. He could take her to a foreign country."

Mrs. Edgerton choked back a sob. "You're right," she said. "We're wasting time. I'm going to hang up, and call the police. I'll call you back after I talk to them."

"I'll get a flight home yet tonight."

There was a click as the call disconnected. Mrs. Edgerton called 911, then told the emergency operator who she was and what had happened. While she waited for the police to arrive, she looked through the house. The front door was open, too. Whoever had been there had left in a hurry.

Mrs. Edgerton called Amy's home.

Mrs. Nordlund answered.

"Is Amy there?"

"No, she isn't. Who's calling, please?"

"This is Elyse Edgerton. Is this Amy's mother?"

"Yes. Isn't she at your house? She left a message that she was going to babysit for you today."

"She did babysit, but when I got home the house was empty and the doors were open. Amy and Kendra are both gone. There's a crudely written, unsigned note from someone who says he or she has Kendra. I'm waiting for the police to arrive."

Mrs. Nordlund sat down, trying to process this information.

"Your daughter was kidnapped while Amy was taking care of her?" Disbelief made Mrs. Nordlund's voice too high. It squeaked on the last word.

"It's possible that both of our daughters were kidnapped. All I know for sure is that Kendra and Amy aren't here and there's a note from someone who claims to have Kendra."

"Does the note mention Amy?"

"No."

"Are there signs of a struggle?"

"No."

"Amy would never let someone she doesn't know into your house."

"Maybe he had a weapon. Maybe the girls were playing outside."

Mrs. Nordlund closed her eyes, not wanting to imagine such a scene.

"Amy's purse is still here," Mrs. Edgerton said.

"What's your address?" Mrs. Nordlund asked. "I'll come over."

As Kendra's mother gave the address, Mrs. Nordlund heard sirens in the background.

"The police are here," Mrs. Edgerton said.

"I'm on my way."

Mrs. Nordlund turned off the oven, grabbed her keys, and rushed out to her car. The last time she had talked to police officers, they had come to her office to tell her that her husband was dead. Could tragedy strike her a second time?

No, she thought. No! Amy's all I have left! Amy had to be okay, and the little Edgerton girl, too. If anything happened to Amy, Mrs. Nordlund didn't think she would be able to go on.

Amy did not recognize the road they were on. She knew they had driven south on Interstate 5, but after they left the freeway, nothing looked familiar. The roads they took got more narrow; the houses more sparse.

"Tubby hungwy," Kendra said. "Tubby want fwench fwies."

"She needs some food," Amy said. "It's her dinnertime."

"Tough," said Smokey.

"We'll be there soon," said Hugh. He looked at Smokey. "Your girlfriend was going to make sure we had food on hand," he said. "If she's out of the picture, did you do it?"

"Not exactly."

"Not exactly? What does that mean? Either you bought food or you didn't."

"When I checked the place last week, there was a jar of peanut butter."

"Tubby like peanut buttah," said Kendra.

"That's all?" said Hugh. "Four of us are supposed to live for a week on one jar of peanut butter?"

"We can buy what we need," Smokey said. "Don't make such a big deal out of it. There's a little store before we reach the turnoff to the cabin."

"Okay, okay. We'll stop there, and you can go in and load up."

"Tubby like tacos," said Kendra.

"What else does Tubby like?" asked Amy. They might as well buy what Kendra would eat. It was going to be hard enough to keep the child happy without offering food she didn't want.

"Tubby like basghetti an' gwill cheese an' pudding."

"Who's this Tubby character?" Smokey asked.

"Her cat," Amy said.

"What cat?" Smokey said. "I'm not wasting money on cat food."

"It isn't a real cat!" Hugh said.

They drove a few minutes in silence.

Hugh said, "If Darielle is on vacation, how are you going to get the DVDs to the Edgertons? You said Darielle would meet you each day and deliver them."

"Not a problem," Smokey said.

"Oh, no? You hadn't thought of that, had you? You never think!"

"I'll mail them," Smokey said.

"That takes too long. Darielle was going to deliver the first one tonight. Even if you film it today, you won't be able to mail it until tomorrow. It'll be Wednesday at the earliest before they get it."

"I could send it FedEx or UPS. They have overnight delivery."

"Oh, brilliant! Great idea! That way the package can be traced to where it was sent from, and the clerk who takes it from you can give the cops a good description. Some of those places even have surveillance cameras in case somebody tries to send a bomb to the President."

"So I'll mail the DVDs. What's the difference if it takes a day or two longer? I can drop them in one of those drive-up boxes in front of the post office."

"This slows us down," Hugh said. "We'll lose a whole day, maybe two."

"Do you have a better suggestion?"

"I do," Amy said. "You could drop us off right now, and then you won't have to worry about mail delivery."

Smokey glared at her in the rearview mirror with such anger that Amy decided she should keep quiet and not annoy him.

"I shoulda said no," Hugh said. "This is the most harebrained scheme I ever heard of, saddling ourselves with two kids for a week while you show off how great you are with your new camcorder. Let's just demand our ransom right away, in the first video."

"We're going to build the suspense," Smokey said. "That's the whole point! Every time the Edgertons get another DVD, they'll be even more anxious to get the kid back. By the time they see the last film, where we tell how much money we want and where they should leave it, they'll agree to anything. If we ask right away, they might say no, and then what'll we do?"

Amy thought it unlikely that Kendra's parents would refuse to pay a ransom immediately, and she didn't see how videos would influence them, but she said nothing. Smokey seemed unbalanced and she knew it would be foolish to disagree with him.

"What about the other kid? You going to put her in the movies, too?"

"Well, sure." Smokey smirked. "Might as well have two sets of parents growing more and more desperate."

Chapter Five

Smokey stopped in front of the Saddle Stop Country Store, a weathered wooden building with a single gas pump out in front and a faded sign advertising ICE COLD COCA-COLA in a glass bottle. Hugh stayed in the car with Amy and Kendra while Smokey went inside.

The store looked as if it had last seen a coat of paint in the 1940s. The windows were full of posters for high school plays from years ago, long-past Fourth of July parades, and handwritten flyers advertising firewood for sale and free kittens. Some of the flyers appeared to have hung there at least as long as the outdated posters.

Amy hoped Smokey would check the expiration dates on anything he bought. She wasn't eager to eat soup that was older than she was.

The store looked like the buildings in those old Western movies that her dad used to love, where the heroes rode horses. "Oaters," he called them. There was even a hitching post near the door.

Smokey returned carrying three full plastic bags, which he stowed in the back of the van. He handed a box of crackers to Hugh when he got back in the car.

"What did you get?" Hugh asked. "I'm starving."

"Corned-beef hash, marshmallows, beef jerky, and crackers."

"Marshmallows?" Hugh said.

"Yeah. I like marshmallows."

"What about milk for the kid?" Hugh asked.

"They were out of milk, but I got beer."

"You can't give beer to a three-year-old," Hugh said.

"I know that. The beer's for me."

"I should have done the shopping."

"I got some other stuff, too," Smokey said. "I'm not stupid."

Amy clamped her lips together to keep from commenting.

"Like what?" asked Hugh.

"Hershey bars."

Hello? Amy thought. How about some oranges or bananas? Maybe a can of peas? She knew fresh salad was too much to expect from the Saddle Stop Country Store—or from Smokey, for that matter—but you'd think he would at least try to provide a balanced diet. Surely the store had cans of apple juice. All little kids like apple juice.

"Marshmallows and Hershey bars," Hugh said.

"What? You don't like Hershey bars?"

Smokey started the engine just as another car came along. It slowed, then pulled in beside them.

"Don't say anything," Hugh warned.

Amy pressed her face against the window, willing the other driver to look her way.

A young man wearing jeans and a denim jacket got out of the car, and glanced toward them. She mouthed the word *help*, hoping he would notice.

Smokey raised one hand casually, as if to say hi to the man. The man nodded in return, then entered the store as Smokey drove away.

Did he even see me? Amy wondered. Did he look closely enough that when my picture's on every newscast tomorrow, he'll remember?

Probably not.

Amy tried to watch for landmarks as they drove on, but everything looked the same. Mile after mile of fields or woods, with an occasional mailbox perched at the entrance of a driveway so long she couldn't see what was at the other end.

Hugh opened the box of crackers, took a few, then handed the box to Amy. She and Kendra ate stale crackers as they rode.

Smokey drove more slowly, although there were no other vehicles on the road, and Amy realized he was watching for a turnoff. When he turned on to a gravel lane that wound off into the trees, Amy unbuckled her seat belt and twisted around to look out the rear window, hoping to see a mailbox or other identifying marker at the end of the lane. She saw only woods.

She buckled up again, wondering where they were. Wherever it was, it didn't get a lot of traffic. Tall weeds grew up through the sparse gravel, and low-hanging branches thumped the top of the car. Vegetation encroached on the sides of the road, so much in some places that Amy wondered how Smokey knew where to steer.

"Slow down," Hugh said. "I can't tell where the road is."

Smokey ignored him.

Dusk descended early in the woods; Smokey turned on the headlights.

The lane curved sharply to the left, and as the car went around the curve there was a loud *clunk*. Amy's head snapped backward as Smokey stomped on the brakes.

Amy saw a tree down across the lane.

"Stupid tree!" Smokey said. "It's right in the middle of the road."

"If you had been driving slower, you could have stopped," Hugh said.

"We'll have to move it," Smokey said.

The two men got out, lifted the tree trunk, and swung the top around until the lane was clear.

When they continued on their way, the car made a loud whining sound. Then it quit running.

"You can fix it, can't you?" Smokey asked. "You're good with engines."

"It's getting dark. Do you have a flashlight?"

"I don't know. Maybe there's one in the glove compartment."

Hugh opened the glove compartment and rooted around inside. "No flashlight," he said. "That figures."

Smokey opened his door. "Okay, everybody out," he said. "We'll walk the rest of the way, and fix the car tomorrow."

Smokey took out the gun.

"What are you doing?" Hugh asked.

"There might be bears in the woods."

"I'm more concerned about Goldilocks," Hugh said, glancing at Kendra.

"How far is it?" Amy asked.

Neither man answered her. She suspected they didn't know.

Hugh and Smokey took the bags of groceries out of the back of the van.

"Tubby go potty," Kendra said.

Amy quickly felt Kendra's overalls, hoping she didn't mean she had already gone. They were dry. "Kendra has to go to the bathroom," Amy said. She had to go, too, but she didn't want to tell the men that.

"She'll have to wait," Smokey said.

"She can't! She's only three years old. When she says she has to go, she means now."

"Tubby go potty!" Kendra said, sounding urgent now.

"Why did I ever agree to this?" Hugh said.

"I'm going to have her go here, next to the lane," Amy said, "so she doesn't wet her pants. We don't have any extra clothes."

"Her clothes!" said Hugh. "Darielle was going to pack what the kid needs for a week."

Smokey said nothing.

"You didn't bring any clothes, did you?" Hugh asked.

"She can wear what she has on," Smokey said.

"What she has on is going to be soaked in about two seconds," Amy said.

"Okay, okay," Hugh said. "Let the kid do what she needs to do."

"She's shy," Amy said. "You'll need to walk on ahead, where you can't see or hear." She had no idea if Kendra cared one way or the other, but she sure didn't want the men knowing that *she* was using the side of the road for a toilet.

"We'll keep walking," Hugh said.

"What if they try to run?" Smokey said.

"Where would we go?" Amy said. "There's no place to run to, and I can't see three feet in front of me."

"Come on," Hugh said. "Get on with it."

The two men moved on, their shapes disappearing quickly in the darkness.

"We're going to go potty right here," Amy told Kendra as she unbuttoned the little girl's overalls. She pulled Kendra's underpants all the way off, and told Kendra to squat.

"Tubby want potty chair," Kendra said.

"There isn't a potty chair here," Amy said. "You'll have to go in the dirt. I'm going to do that, too."

She waited until Kendra was finished. Then, hoping that the men did not decide to come back to check on her, Amy quickly relieved herself.

She found a tissue in her pocket, tore it in half, and used half to wipe Kendra and half for herself. She threw the tissue away. She felt guilty for littering, but she wasn't going to put it back in her pocket. She longed for some soap and hot water to wash her hands.

She pulled up her own clothes, and got Kendra dressed again. Then they started down the dark lane in the direction Hugh and Smokey had gone. She could hear their voices ahead. It sounded as if they were arguing again.

Kendra walked slower and slower; Amy realized the child was frightened. She picked Kendra up and carried her.

"Hurry up!" Smokey called. "What's taking you so long?"

"I have to carry Kendra," Amy called back, "and she's heavy."

To her surprise, Hugh returned. "I'll carry her," he said, relieving Amy of her burden. Kendra laid her head on Hugh's shoulder. One hand clutched Tubby; the other went around Hugh's neck. Amy wondered if Kendra had done that when Smokey lifted her from her bed.

Mrs. Edgerton was right, Amy thought. Kendra is a little sweetheart, and I need to keep her safe.

Their destination turned out to be an old cabin, the kind used as temporary lodging by hunters or skiers. A clay flowerpot stood beside the front door. Smokey removed a key from underneath it, and opened the door. They all trooped in. The cabin smelled musty, as if it had been closed up for a long time.

"Where's the light switch?" Hugh asked.

"Uh, there isn't one," Smokey said.

"You're telling me this dump doesn't have electricity?" Hugh said. "How are we gonna cook that hash?"

"There's a fireplace," Smokey said. "We're going to cook over the fire."

Amy could hear him fumbling about in the dark.

"Here it is," Smokey said. "You got any matches, Hugh?"

"Now, why would I be carrying around matches? You're the one who smokes."

"Oh. Right."

Amy heard a clicking noise, and then a tiny flame made a small circle of light as Smokey held up a cigarette lighter.

"Looks like we need to bring in some firewood," Smokey said.

"Figures," said Hugh. "We'll probably need to chop the tree down, too, and saw it into logs."

"Naw," said Smokey. "There's a big stack of wood around back."

Hugh set Kendra on the floor. The little girl clung to Amy's hand. "Tubby want Mommy," she said.

"Mommy can't come right now," Amy said. "Pretend that I'm your mommy."

Smokey managed to get a fire started. The firelight revealed a small wall-hung cupboard that held a flashlight, a half-full jar of peanut butter, and a deck of cards. An empty cracker box with a large hole chewed in it lay on the floor under the cupboard, amid crumbs and mouse droppings.

With no utensils to cook in, dinner was a disaster. Smokey tried to spear a hunk of the hash on a stick, to roast it, but it dropped off into the flames, sizzling and spitting as the fat hit the fire.

"Tubby want basghetti," Kendra said.

"Right," said Hugh. "We all want spaghetti, with Caesar salad and a side of garlic toast."

"Keep that kid quiet!" Smokey said.

"She's hungry," Amy said. "It's way past her usual dinnertime and all she's had is a few crackers."

Hugh picked up one of the plastic bags from the Saddle Stop Country Store and handed it to Amy.

"Is there a sink in here?" Amy asked. "We need to wash our hands."

Smokey exploded. "La-di-dah! So the two princesses have to wash their dainty little hands before they eat! Oh, we wouldn't want them to get any germs, now, would we?"

He seemed so furious over her question that Amy quickly mumbled, "Never mind. It's okay."

She reached in the bag and pulled out a can of tomato soup. It wasn't much use without a pan to heat it in or spoons to eat with.

In the end, Amy and Kendra ate beef jerky and some more stale crackers for dinner, followed by a Hershey bar, which they split. When they had finished, Amy said, "I'm going to put Kendra to bed."

"No!" Smokey said. "She can't go to sleep yet. I'm going to take some video of her."

"Well, get on with it," Hugh said.

Smokey hesitated.

"What?" said Hugh.

"My camcorder's in the car."

"Figures," said Hugh.

"I'll go get it," Smokey said. "I'll be right back." He picked up the small flashlight that they'd found in the cupboard.

"Forget it," Hugh said. "Until I get the car fixed, you can't mail a DVD anyway. You might as well wait until morning. You can shoot the video while I work on the car."

"My new camcorder is so cool," Smokey said. "It records directly to a DVD that we can mail to the kid's parents."

"How much did that set you back?" Hugh asked.

"Nothing. I charged it."

"You still have to pay eventually."

"Not when the credit card's stolen."

"Where do you want us to sleep?" Amy asked. The cabin contained only a crude wooden table and two chairs. There were no beds, or even fold-up cots.

"We should have brought sleeping bags," Hugh said. "Why didn't you tell me there weren't any beds?"

"There are blankets," Smokey said, pointing to a pile in the corner. "We don't need beds."

"I need to take Kendra to the bathroom before we go to bed," Amy said. "Where is it?"

"Out the door and turn left," Smokey said. "Behind the cabin."

"Take the flashlight," Hugh said.

Amy took Kendra's hand. "We're going to go potty," she said. "It's a new kind of potty that's kept outside."

Using the flashlight, she found the small building where Smokey had said it would be.

Praying it wasn't full of spiders, Amy opened the door.

"Yuck," said Kendra. "Potty stink."

"It sure does," Amy agreed. She shined the light across the rough wooden seat with its crudely cut hole. At least the outhouse contained toilet paper, which was more than Amy had expected. Too bad it didn't also have some air freshener.

"You're a good girl, Kendra," Amy said as they started back toward the cabin. "Tomorrow I'm going to tell you a story and play a game with you."

Amy's grandma had told her that everyone needs to anticipate happy times. When Amy's dad died, Grandma had said, "No matter how sad you feel, plan something special that you want to do each day, even if it's only taking a bubble bath or watching a movie. Set a date to visit a friend, or order a book you want to read from the library. Always have something to look forward to."

It had been good advice, and Amy intended to do that now with Kendra. If the little girl always expected something fun to happen, it would make the time here in this awful cabin, away from her parents, seem easier.

"Tubby like games," Kendra said.

Back inside, Amy plucked the top blanket from the heap. It smelled like the insides of old sneakers on a hot day. She didn't even want to think about who had used it since it was last laundered, if, indeed, it had ever been washed.

Recalling the mouse droppings, she took the blanket outside and shook it before spreading it on the floor. She saw no pillows, and didn't ask.

"We're going to sleep together," she told Kendra.

"Tubby need jammies," Kendra said.

"Not tonight," Amy said. "This is a camping trip, and we get to sleep in our clothes."

She removed Kendra's shoes, then had the child lie toward the middle of the blanket. After making sure Tubby was comfortable, Amy lay down beside Kendra, then pulled the rest of the blanket over the top of both of them. It will do, she thought. At least we're warm and we'll be dry if it rains.

Kendra fell asleep quickly, but Amy, despite her weariness, lay awake. Her mind rewound and played back the day's events, trying to figure out what she could do to get herself and Kendra safely out of this predicament.

Chapter Six

They seemed to be miles from any other people, so the chances of being heard if she screamed for help were zero. She considered writing *Help! Kendra and Amy* in the dirt on the back of the van so that when Smokey went to mail the movie, someone would see it. But what if Hugh or Smokey saw it first?

Hugh already seemed taut as a stretched rubber band, as if he might snap in two at any moment. Smokey didn't act nervous, but he had a coldness, an underlying anger that made Amy afraid to cross him. Remembering how he had reacted when she asked about water to wash with, she sensed he could get violent quickly, with little provocation.

Amy decided Smokey's videos were her best chance—probably her only chance—of getting help. Somehow she had to plant clues in those films, clues that would help the police find her. Of course she had to do it in such a way that Hugh and Smokey didn't catch on to what she was up to. If they got suspicious of her, there was no telling what they would do.

Amy lay awake as the others slept, trying to figure out a way to send secret messages via Smokey's DVDs. She was drifting off to sleep, in that halfway state between being awake and being sound asleep, when it hit her. She often used that falling-asleep time to think about the story she was writing, mulling it over in her mind, hoping her subconscious would continue to work on it while she slept. Maybe that's why "Winning Secrets" popped into her head now, presenting her with a way to send clues.

Amy's eyes flew open. She would use the method that she had devised for her story characters. In the story, her character scratched first one ear and then the other, as a signal that his next word was the secret clue.

Amy's best friend, Jorja, had read "Winning Secrets." While Smokey was filming her, Amy would scratch one ear and then scratch the other, and next she would give the clue. As soon as Jorja saw the DVDs, she would figure out the signal.

Amy was certain that Jorja would see the DVDs that Smokey made. They would be big news, and the networks would play them again and again on TV, for the whole world to see. This would work!

Amy was wide-awake now, excited by her plan. Of course she still had to figure out what the clues would be. They had to be subtle so that Hugh and Smokey didn't catch on.

Tomorrow she would begin scratching her ears now and then, even when Smokey wasn't filming her, so that the men got used to the scratching and didn't realize that it was a signal.

Amy's mind raced as she tried to work out potential clues. She decided the car should be her first clue. If the police knew what kind of car to look for, they might spot Smokey when he went to town to mail the DVDs. She remembered a boy in Missouri who had been abducted, and the abductor got caught because somebody told the police about a truck he'd seen in the area at the time the boy disappeared. When the police spotted the truck, they found the missing boy.

What other clues could she send? She couldn't remember what Smokey had said his last name was, when he was bragging to Hugh about making the videos. Henderson? Anderson? Something like that, but she wasn't sure. Maybe she could learn the last names of the men and somehow turn those into clues.

What else? There was the Saddle Stop Country Store. That would lead the police to look in this area, but as hard as she tried, she couldn't think of a way to turn that into a clue and sneak it into the film.

Jorja's head ached, and her nose was stuffed up from crying so much. Ever since Amy's mom had called to ask if she had talked to Amy that day, Jorja had felt as if she were living in a nightmare. How could this bc? How could her best friend since third grade be missing?

Even after Jorja saw Amy's picture on television, along with Kendra Edgerton's picture, it still felt unreal. An Amber Alert had gone out for both girls, but the police admitted they had no suspect in the case and no clues. They had no idea what kind of vehicle they were looking for, either.

Every news channel featured Mrs. Edgerton tearfully pleading for her daughter's kidnapper to release her. "Drop the girls at a safe place, such as a hospital," she said.

Mrs. Nordlund, struggling to maintain control, said she did not know who would have done this, or where the girls might have been taken. She begged anyone with information to come forward.

By the eleven o'clock news, a $20,000 reward had been posted for any information leading to the safe return of Kendra Edgerton and Amy Nordlund. Police dogs had searched the Edgerton property, but always lost the scent at the curb, making authorities think the girls had been taken away in a vehicle.

No neighbor had seen a car or anyone suspicious-looking in the area. No one had heard anything unusual. Mr. Edgerton was home now; he couldn't think of anyone who might have taken his daughter. He said he and his wife had no enemies. No disgruntled employees had been fired. The Edgertons had not been involved in any court case or dispute.

Mr. and Mrs. Edgerton stood hand in hand during the latest interview. They looked at each other frequently, and it was clear that they loved each other as well as their daughter. In their terrible fear, they supported each other.

It struck Jorja that, in contrast, Mrs. Nordlund seemed achingly alone. She had no husband to help her through this, and Jorja knew that Amy's grandparents lived in another state. The person whom Mrs. Nordlund loved most, and who would normally be at her side in a crisis, was Amy.

Jorja splashed cold water on her face and went downstairs, where her own parents were still watching a local channel, hoping for good news. "I think I should stay at Amy's house tonight," Jorja said.

Her mother looked startled.

"Her mom's probably there all alone," Jorja said. "I think someone should be with her."

"I don't know, honey," Jorja's mom said. "We don't want to intrude. Besides, it's almost midnight; it's too late to call."

"I wouldn't get in the way. If Mrs. Nordlund needed to go somewhere, like to the police station or something, I'd be there to answer the phone in case Amy called."

Her parents looked uncertainly at each other.

"It isn't too late to call," Jorja said. "Her mom won't be sleeping. Not with Amy missing."

"She has a point," her dad said. "Amy's mother is probably pacing the floor and looking out the window."

"I could sleep in Amy's room," Jorja said.

Jorja's mom nodded. "All right. Call Mrs. Nordlund and ask her if she wants you to come."

"Oh, Jorja," Mrs. Nordlund said. "Yes, I'd love to have you here. Are you sure it's okay with your parents? I'd better talk to one of them."

Jorja handed the phone to her mother, and the arrangements were quickly made. Twenty minutes later, Jorja was sitting at the Nordlunds' kitchen table, drinking hot chocolate and hearing about the call from Mrs. Edgerton and everything that had happened since.

"They are nice people," Mrs. Nordlund told Jorja. "They never once suggested any of this was Amy's fault, which of course it isn't, but still it would be only human nature to wonder if their regular sitter might somehow have prevented this from happening. Instead they seem as worried about Amy as they are about Kendra, and the reward they posted is contingent on both girls being safely returned, not just their own daughter."

"I wish I could help somehow," Jorja said. "I feel so powerless."

"You are helping," Mrs. Nordlund said. "Thank you for being here tonight."

As Jorja rinsed her mug, Mrs. Nordlund said, "I suppose we should both try to get some sleep. The police have promised to let me know if they learn anything."

Jorja put her pajamas on and got into Amy's bed. She had slept in this room many times before, but never by herself. Always in the past when she stayed overnight, she and Amy had talked, and laughed, and told secrets in the dark. Now the room seemed too still, too empty. She wondered where her friend was, and what she was doing.

Jorja looked at the pictures on Amy's bulletin board: her mom and dad, her grandparents, lots of photos with Jorja. The certificate from the community center, stating that Amy had completed the babysitting course, was tacked to the bottom, and Amy's gymnastics medals hung in a bright row across the top. A brief newspaper clipping from last year, when Amy had won a citywide essay contest, occupied the center spot.

Amy dreamed of being a writer. She kept an "ideas box" full of newspaper clippings, snatches of conversation, and other items that she thought she might be able to use in her writing. She even had one entire notebook containing only descriptions that she had written.

"I love to write descriptions," she had told Jorja. "Someday when I'm writing books, I'll be able to flip open this notebook and find exactly the description I need, just waiting for me to use it."

Jorja had looked at the description notebook. She wondered how Amy could think it was fun to write long sentences about puddles and falling leaves and whipped cream, but she had to admit Amy's words painted pictures in her mind.

Books lined Amy's shelves and spilled onto the surface of her dresser. Two were on the bedside table, with bookmarks inserted.

Amy's fat green notebook, where she currently wrote her stories, also lay on the bedside table. A pang of guilt hit Jorja when she saw it. Amy had loaned the notebook to her, saying, "I like the story I'm working on. Why don't you take it home and read it, and tell me what you think?"

Jorja had taken the precious notebook home with her and had glanced at the new work—"Winning Secrets." It looked interesting, but it was already thirty pages long, and her favorite TV show was on that night. She never got around to reading the story. Not wanting to admit to Amy that she had not bothered to read something so important to her, Jorja had returned the notebook the next day, saying, "I think this will be your best story yet."

Amy had beamed. "Do you really think so? It's not too unbelievable?"

"The only thing unbelievable," Jorja had replied, "is how you think up all this stuff."

She shivered now, even though it wasn't cold in Amy's room. Where was her friend? What was happening to her tonight?

DAY TWO

Chapter Seven

The next morning, as she and Kendra ate crackers and marshmallows for breakfast, Amy scratched her ears, first the right and then the left. A few minutes later, she did it again.

"You got mosquito bites?" Hugh asked. "You shouldn't scratch at mosquito bites."

"It's allergies," Amy said. "When I'm in a lot of trees, my ears itch."

She hoped he wouldn't tell her not to scratch again.

Hugh said nothing more about it, even though Amy continued to rub her ears every few minutes.

When Hugh and Smokey headed back to the car, Amy and Kendra walked along. Amy wanted to find out what kind of vehicle it was so she could make up the first clue.

The walk in daylight didn't take as long as it had the night before, and Kendra didn't have to be carried. If Amy had been there under other circumstances, she would have enjoyed strolling through the woods. Kendra kept stopping to examine stones and leaves, and once, when Amy pointed out a squirrel, Kendra said, "Tubby like," and ran toward it, which, of course, sent the squirrel scampering in the other direction.

While Smokey got his camcorder and Hugh looked at the engine, Amy examined the vehicle. She didn't know much about cars. Except for knowing this was a small van, she could not have described it. Now she noted the color, and was dismayed to see that the back windows were tinted. The young man outside the store yesterday probably never saw her. She walked to the back of the van to look for a logo.

Yes. She saw it. This was a Dodge Caravan.

"What are you doing?" Hugh said.

"Nothing," Amy said, looking quickly away from the van. "I'm just waiting for you."

"You were looking pretty hard at the license plate," Hugh said. "If you're thinking of memorizing it and turning it in to the cops later, you can forget it."

"That's right," Smokey said. "You won't be telling the cops anything."

Amy hadn't thought of memorizing the license-plate number, but now she realized she should. She walked away from the van, but glanced back long enough to see the license plate. She repeated it to herself several times.

"These plates won't trace back to us anyway," Smokey said. "They'll lead to whoever owns the van."

"You talk too much," Hugh said. "Go make your video."

Amy was glad to learn that the van was stolen. That meant the police were probably already looking for it. Now she needed to let them know that the stolen van was connected to the kidnapping.

As Amy and Kendra followed Smokey back to the cabin, Amy mulled over ways to sneak that information into the film. She couldn't think of any way to work the license plate number into what she said. Hugh and Smokey would never allow that. By the time they got inside, Amy knew what she would say to let the police know what kind of vehicle to look for.

"You two stand over there by the window," Smokey directed.

“When I point at you, start talking. Tell them who you are and say that you’re okay. Tell them we’re treating you good.” He nodded toward Kendra. “Have the kid say something to her parents.”

Amy took Kendra’s hand and led her toward the window. “We’re going to make a video,” she said, “to send to Mommy and Daddy. Maybe Tubby could wave to them, and say hi.”

The two girls faced Smokey and waited while he fooled around with the camcorder’s settings. Finally he pointed, and said, “Go.”

“I’m Amy Nordlund,” Amy said, “and this is Kendra Edgerton. As you can see, we’re okay.” She leaned down to Kendra and said, “What do you want to tell your mommy and daddy?”

Kendra said, “Tubby eat candy.” She held up the toy cat.

“Kendra misses you,” Amy said, “but I’m with her all the time and I’m taking care of her.”

“Tubby need jammies,” Kendra said.

Amy scratched at her right ear and then at her left ear. “Tell Aunt Cara and Uncle Van not to worry,” she said, “and also Mrs. White. I hope we’ll see all of you again soon.”

Her palms felt sweaty. Smokey kept the camcorder pointed at her. Emboldened, Amy scratched her ears again, then said, “I wish I had my story notebook with me.”

She paused.

“Keep going,” Smokey said. “That’s too short.”

“I don’t know what else to say.”

“Have the kid talk more. Say you want to go home.”

Amy said, “Kendra, why don’t you tell about our bed?”

Kendra shook her head.

“We have a blanket,” Amy said, “and we slept together. We weren’t cold last night, but we want to come home.”

“Tubby want Mommy,” Kendra said. Her bottom lip quivered.

For the first time, Amy saw Smokey's mouth curve into a smile, although the smile didn't make it from his lips to his eyes. "Perfect," he said.

On that happy note, Smokey ended the video.

Hugh returned. "The car's running again," he said. "A wire had been jarred loose, probably when you hit that tree. Did you make the film?"

"Want to see it?" Smokey asked.

Amy hoped Hugh would say no. She was pretty sure Smokey wouldn't catch on to her clues, but Hugh seemed smarter, and more suspicious. He would likely question everything she said. What if he figured out that Aunt Cara, Uncle Van, and Mrs. White were a message to the police?

"Yes," Hugh said. "I want to see all the videos before you mail them."

Smokey played back the video while Hugh watched over his shoulder. Amy couldn't see the tiny screen, which was only about two inches wide, but she could hear the sound. She held her breath at the part about Aunt Cara, Uncle Van, and Mrs. White, but Hugh didn't say anything until the film ended.

"Who's Mrs. White?" he asked.

"My teacher."

"You need to give the parents their instructions," he told Smokey.

Smokey turned the camcorder back on, pointing it at Kendra and Tubby. "You'll get another DVD tomorrow," he said. "Until then, do nothing. Do not call the police." He turned the camcorder off, and said, "Time to get this in the mail."

Hugh said, "While you're out, buy a pan to cook in and some paper plates and plastic forks. And get some coffee."

"I don't like coffee."

"Well, I do."

"It'll be cold before I get back here."

"I don't mean buy a cup of coffee," Hugh said. "Buy a package of coffee, and a pot to make it in so I can brew it myself."

"Hot dogs and buns would be good," Amy suggested. "We could roast hot dogs on sticks."

"Tubby like hot dog," said Kendra.

"I'll need money," Smokey said, "in case a stop has been put on the last credit card."

Hugh rolled his eyes and handed Smokey some cash. "Don't talk to anybody," he instructed. "Don't waste any time. Just do what you're supposed to do and get back here."

"What?" Smokey said. "You think I'm going to get in a poker game or shoot some pool?"

"Just don't say anything. And buy a newspaper, if you see one."

Smokey picked up the camcorder.

"Why are you taking that?" Hugh asked.

"I can recharge the battery in the car. It plugs into the cigarette lighter."

As Smokey opened the cabin door, Hugh said, "Where's your gun?"

Smokey patted his pocket.

"Leave it here, in case you get pulled over."

"I won't get pulled over. Why would I get pulled over?"

Hugh shrugged. "I've seen how you drive," he said.

"It's my gun. It's going with me."

"At least put it in the glove compartment, and leave it there."

They all watched Smokey drive off. Hugh muttered, "He may be my nephew, but he's still stupid as a stump."

Amy didn't reply. The first DVD was on its way, with her clues in it. Jorja would see it as early as tomorrow. By the time Smokey goes to town to mail the second film, police all over the state might be on the look out for a white Dodge Caravan. It made her feel less helpless to know that, so far, her plan had worked.

"I found the well," Hugh said. "The pump still works. The water's kind of rusty, but that'll clear up after we use it a while."

He led Amy to an old iron pump that stood in a clearing off to the side of the cabin. Weeds had taken over now, so tall that the pump had not been visible until Hugh pulled them away.

Amy pumped the handle. It creaked its resistance at first, then moved more easily. A trickle of reddish-colored water emerged from the spout. Kendra clapped her hands in delight. "Watah!" she cried, and stuck her hands into the flow.

"That's right," Amy said. "Water. You can wash your hands and face." She watched as Kendra rubbed water on her face, removing the smears of chocolate that ringed her mouth.

"Tubby do," Kendra said, and grabbed the pump handle, but it was too hard for her and the water stopped.

"I'll pump for you," Hugh said.

"Thanks."

He worked the handle up and down while Amy washed her hands and face. Even without soap, she felt cleaner.

"Do you think it's safe to drink?" she asked.

"Probably safer than what comes out of your faucet at home. No pollutants out in the country; nobody spraying their lawns with pesticides or dumping paint thinner in the dirt."

"If Smokey brings back some pots," she said, "we can catch the water and have it inside."

"Don't count on Smokey to bring anything useful. I just hope he doesn't get picked up for reckless driving."

"Why are you doing this with him when he's so undependable?"

"I was in a room with no doors, no way out," Hugh said. "Smokey opened a window and I decided to climb through."

Amy wasn't certain what he meant by that. "Will you really let Kendra go?" she asked.

"That's the deal. I told him I wouldn't help unless we give the kid back unharmed."

Amy wasn't sure whether to push her luck by asking the next question, but she needed to know. "What about me?" she said. "Will you let me go, too?"

He stared at her for a moment. "I did time in prison," he said, "and I'm not going back, ever."

"What about Smokey?"

Hugh looked away. "Smokey's a firecracker with a short fuse. Try not to set him off."

Chapter Eight

While Kendra poked in the dirt with a stick, Amy tried to figure out what her next clue could be. She brainstormed silently, the way she did when she tried to figure out story ideas, letting words drop into her mind quickly, one after the other, like beads sliding from a string. She paused on the word *nanny*.

Kendra's nanny knew all about the kidnapping plan, but since she was on vacation, Amy wondered if the police would question her. Somehow Amy had to let them know that the nanny, Darielle something, had been Smokey's girlfriend, and was going to get part of the ransom money. But how?

Amy knew she should prepare for the second video. Smokey might want to shoot it yet today, and she needed to be sure she was ready. Nanny. Nanny.

While her mind searched for a way to give a clue, Amy heard the birds chirping in the woods, and the high chittering of a squirrel. That gave her the idea she needed.

"You're going to learn the animal sounds," Amy said.

"Tubby like animals," Kendra said.

"This is a fun new game," Amy said. "I'll ask you what the animal says, and then you and Tubby tell me the answer. If you don't know, I'll teach you, and pretty soon you'll be able to make all the animal noises."

"Okay."

"What does the baby cat say?" Amy asked.

"Tubby be cat."

"Yes, Tubby's a cat. What does Tubby say?"

"Meow," said Kendra. "Meow, meow."

"Good!" Amy said, and Kendra beamed.

"What does the daddy dog say?"

Kendra thought a minute. "Woof?" she asked.

Amy nodded. "Woof, woof," she said.

"Woof, woof," Kendra repeated.

"That's right."

Amy taught Kendra that the baby chicken says, "Peep, peep," and the daddy donkey says, "Heehaw, heehaw."

Kendra liked that one. "Heehaw!" she shouted. "Heehaw, heehaw, heehaw!"

Then Amy came to the whole point of the game.

"What does the *mama goat* say?" she asked. She stressed the words mama goat as she asked the question.

Kendra didn't know.

"The mama goat says naaa, naaa," Amy said.

"Naaa, naaa," said Kendra.

"Good!"

Then Amy started over, repeating all of the animals. Twice while they played, she scratched both ears, just in case Hugh was watching.

Kendra was a quick learner and could soon make all the animal sounds perfectly. Of course, for Amy's purposes, it didn't matter whether Kendra remembered correctly or not. All that counted was for Jorja to realize Amy was sending the clue signal before she said, "Mama goat."

If Jorja caught that, someone would surely figure out that a mama goat was also called a nanny goat, and then the police detectives would go the next step and question Kendra's nanny.

Or would they? Amy remembered countless games of charades where the person acting out a word was positive the clues were clear, while those trying to figure out the word had no idea what the actor was trying to convey.

The same thing happened in that game where you draw a picture to try to get the others to say a particular word. When you *know* what the word is, the drawing seems obvious, but when you don't know, it isn't so easy.

What if nobody caught on that *mama goat* meant the police should talk to Kendra's nanny?

What if Jorja didn't make the connection between the ear scratching and "Winning Secrets"? In that case, it wouldn't matter how great Amy's clues were.

Detective Rockport and the other police detectives combed every inch of the Edgerton home again. His squad had dusted for fingerprints and interviewed neighbors the night before.

The lots in the Edgertons' neighborhood were all three or more acres—not the sort of area where you chatted often across the back fence. The neighbors on both sides and across the street had been gone all afternoon on the day of the kidnapping. Even if the babysitter had shouted for help, no one would have heard her.

"We got two clear sets of fingerprints other than yours from the front door and from the kitchen phone," Detective Rockport told the Edgertons, the morning after the kidnapping. "One set is Amy's; they match prints lifted from her bedroom. The other set is probably the kidnapper, but they don't match any prints that were in the system."

"So whoever took Kendra does not have a criminal record?" Mr. Edgerton asked.

"That's right."

"Good," Mrs. Edgerton said. "At least he isn't a hardened crook." Somehow, that made her feel better.

Detective Rockport would have been happier if the prints had matched someone who had been arrested before so he'd know who to look for. As it was, the kidnapper could be anyone.

Now what? Amy thought. She would practice the animal sounds with Kendra again later on, but she didn't want to overdo it and have Kendra get tired of the game before Smokey filmed it.

"Tubby hungwy," Kendra said.

"Me, too," said Amy as she stood. "Let's go inside and get a snack."

As she approached the cabin door, she heard an odd sound. She hesitated, then realized it was Hugh snoring.

Amy put her finger to her lips, and Kendra nodded. She seemed to understand that she should be quiet.

Maybe we should try to run for it, Amy thought. Smokey won't be back for a while. If we follow the lane, we wouldn't get lost and we could hide if I heard the white van coming. Eventually we'd get to the bigger road. She didn't know how far it was to the Saddle Stop Country Store, but only a few miles. She was sure they could make it.

Amy breathed faster as she considered what to do. Hugh might not wake up until Smokey returned. She and Kendra would have a good head start. Of course, once Smokey got back, the men would use the car, but it should be easy to hide in the dense woods. The car tires made a lot of noise on the gravel last night; she would hear it coming in time to get out of sight.

She would need to take food and water. Amy whispered, "You and Tubby wait here and be very quiet so we don't wake up Hugh. I'll bring our snack out."

Kendra nodded solemnly, and sat down.

Amy slipped inside the cabin. Hugh was slumped in a chair, his mouth slightly open. Amy picked up one of the plastic bags. It made a crinkling sound and she stopped, holding her breath as she watched Hugh.

He let out another snore. Amy looked in the bag. It contained a package of beef jerky, two chocolate bars, and a bottle of water. It would have to do.

She tiptoed outside, then motioned for Kendra to follow her. She walked quickly away from the cabin with Kendra at her heels. When she reached the edge of the woods, she looked back. The cabin door was closed.

Wishing she had her backpack, she unbuckled her belt, slipped it through the handles of the bag, and rebuckled it. The water bottle bounced against her thigh when she walked, but it left her hands free in case she had to carry Kendra part of the way.

She unwrapped one of the chocolate bars and gave a piece to Kendra. "Shh," she whispered. "We still have to be quiet."

Kendra popped the chocolate in her mouth. Amy took her hand and walked farther away from the cabin.

When they were far enough that she was sure Hugh wouldn't hear her voice, she said, "Do you know how to play hide-and-seek?"

"Tubby hide good. Tubby hide in bathtub."

"We don't have a bathtub here," Amy said, "but we're going to hide from Hugh and Smokey. We're going to run fast, and hide where they can't find us."

"Okay."

I hope I'm doing the right thing, Amy thought. If we go back now, he'll never know we left. He won't be angry. But if we try to get away, and they catch us . . . Her thought trailed off. She didn't know what would happen then. She didn't even want to think about it.

Still, it didn't seem smart to stay at the cabin and make no attempt to escape. Her clues might not work. She and Kendra might not be found. What was going to happen after Smokey mailed the last film, the one where he planned to demand money in exchange for Kendra?

If Mr. and Mrs. Edgerton paid the ransom, Hugh and Smokey might let Kendra go, or they might not. Kidnappers did that sometimes; they demanded a ransom, but when they got it, they killed the child anyway.

Even if they released Kendra, what about Amy? They knew she could identify them, and her mom didn't have any money for a ransom. When Smokey said, "You won't be telling anything to the police later," he meant she'd be dead.

Amy shuddered. Unless Hugh intervened, Smokey would shoot her. She couldn't depend on Hugh to save her. She had to save herself.

I'm making the right choice, Amy decided. I have to get away, if I can.

She suspected the only reason the men didn't get rid of her right away was that it was easier for them to let her take care of Kendra. If she wasn't there, they would have to deal with "Tubby go potty" themselves.

It's hard to be responsible for a small child, Amy thought. There's never any time off. She hadn't realized until now how difficult it was to be a parent.

Kendra ran for only a few minutes. Then she said, "Tubby west now."

"We don't have to run all the time," Amy said. "We can walk for a while, but we do have to keep moving."

Walk to Kendra meant ambling along, showing Tubby the pretty weeds, stopping to watch a caterpillar.

Amy's nerves were on edge. She wanted to hurry the little girl, but she didn't want to frighten her. She couldn't say, "We have to run because those men are bad and if they find us they might hurt us."

Instead, she kept looking for something ahead that would interest Kendra. Then Amy would point and say, "Oh, look. There's a pinecone," or "I see a bush with red berries on it." That got Kendra moving, at least far enough to examine whatever Amy had pointed out.

Amy knew she couldn't assume that Hugh would sleep until Smokey got back. There was a chance he had already awakened and was running after her and Kendra while they dawdled along.

As she looked ahead for something else to interest Kendra and get her to hurry, Amy spotted a pile of horse nuggets. They were dry, as if they'd been there a while, but still it meant someone on horseback had passed this way, and if they rode through here once, they might come again.

Maybe the cabin was not as far out in the wilderness as it seemed. Or maybe someone occasionally brought a horse here in a horse trailer, then rode on the gravel lane. Either way, it gave her hope that someone besides Hugh and Smokey knew about this lane, and the cabin.

"Do you want me to carry you for a while?" Amy asked.

Kendra nodded. "Tubby, too," she said.

Amy picked up the little girl. She knew she'd get tired a lot sooner herself this way, but it was also going to be faster than trying to get Kendra to hurry. Amy didn't run, but she strode along quickly, shifting Kendra from one hip to the other every five minutes or so.

She listened as she walked, straining to hear any sound either behind her or coming toward her. If Hugh realized the girls were gone, he would run after them, and she was pretty sure she'd hear his footsteps.

It seemed too soon for the van to return, but she couldn't know for sure, so she looked as far ahead as she could, hoping she would hear or see a vehicle before the driver noticed her.

Chapter Nine

Smokey stopped first at the Saddle Stop Country Store. He asked for a mailing bag that he could use to send the DVD in, but the Saddle Stop carried fishing tackle, cold drinks, and potato chips, not office supplies. Well, he had to find a post office, anyway. He'd buy a mailer when he got to town.

It took longer than he had thought it would, but he located a store that sold padded envelopes and bought seven the right size. He asked the clerk where the closest post office was, and she told him how to get there.

Back in the car, Smokey put the DVD in an envelope and sealed it. He had a moment of panic when he feared he had left the paper with the Edgertons' address on it back at the cabin, but he found it on the car floor. He didn't have anything to write with, so he went back in the store and bought a pen.

When he found the post office, he couldn't drop the DVD in the box out in front because he didn't have any stamps on it. He went inside and got in line. While he waited, he noticed that the post office sold mailing bags. He could have come straight here.

As soon as he got back to the car after mailing the DVD, he realized he should have bought extra stamps so that he could drop the rest of the DVDs into the outside box. He returned, stood in line again, and said, "I want enough stamps to mail six more packages exactly like the one I just mailed."

"How much was it?" the clerk asked.

"A dollar ninety-two."

She counted out the stamps, and Smokey paid her. He returned to the car, feeling on top of the world. He had bought enough mailing bags and stamps. He had thought of everything. Hugh couldn't accuse him of being stupid, or of not planning ahead. Just because Hugh was twenty years older than Smokey, he always thought he should be in charge. Well, not this time. This was Smokey's idea and his camcorder, and he was the boss.

Smokey's next stop was a grocery store. He put hot dogs and buns in the cart, along with cheese, crackers, a jar of grape jelly, and a loaf of bread. He paused. What else was it Hugh had wanted?

Oh, yeah. Coffee. Smokey found the coffee aisle. He couldn't believe how many different kinds there were. Having no idea what Hugh would want, he grabbed a small bag and threw it in the cart. He found a saucepan, but not a coffeepot. Hugh would have to boil his coffee in the pan.

The store had a deli, so Smokey got himself an order of chicken wings. He paid for that separately, in case Hugh checked the grocery receipt. He ate his chicken at a little table near the deli section. Someone had left a newspaper there, and when Smokey picked it up to move it, he saw the front-page headline:

EDGERTON DAUGHTER AND BABYSITTER KIDNAPPED

Smokey clenched his jaw. The Edgertons had called the police. They had disobeyed his instructions.

Smokey skimmed the article. At the end it said, *Police have no clues to the kidnapper. Anyone with information is asked to call 911.* Angrily, Smokey folded the newspaper and took it with him.

He had planned to return the kid unharmed, but now that the cops had been called, all bets were off.

• • •

Amy's arms ached, and she was thirsty. She set Kendra down, then opened the bottle of water.

"Tubby want dwink," Kendra said.

Amy handed her the bottle, and Kendra took several sips, managing to spill some on the front of her shirt. She pretended to give the toy cat a drink, too, and then gave the bottle back to Amy.

Although it wasn't cold, the water refreshed Amy. "Let's go," she said, and she picked Kendra up again. They had gone only a few feet when Kendra said, "Tubby go potty," and Amy knew she couldn't postpone that. She had been lucky so far; Kendra had not had an accident, and Amy wanted to keep it that way.

Amy tried to make a game of using a leaf instead of toilet paper.

As they continued down the road, Amy wondered again if running away was the right thing to do. She wished she could ask Mom for advice. She thought about her dad, too, and talked to him in her head. I may not be making the wisest decisions, Dad, she thought, but I'm giving it my best shot. I'm taking care of Kendra and I sent clues about the van in the DVD. I'm trying hard to save us both, and that's as responsible as I know how to be.

Hugh opened his eyes and sat up, rubbing his stiff neck and silently cursing Smokey for not outfitting the cabin properly. They needed air mattresses or cots. No wonder he fell asleep in his chair; he hadn't slept well the night before. How could he, lying on a hard floor, with no pillow?

Hugh stood and stretched, working the kinks out. He hadn't meant to fall asleep. He walked to the cabin door and opened it. When he had last looked out at the two girls, they were sitting in the sun playing some kind of word game. Now the patch of sun was gone. So were the girls.

Hugh hurried outside. Maybe she had taken the little kid to the outhouse again. Kendra said, "Tubby go potty," about every half hour, and Amy would rush outside with her. Kendra must have a bladder the size of a marble.

He flung open the outhouse door. It was empty.

Hugh turned back to the cabin. "Amy!" he called. "Where are you?"

No answer.

Back inside, he looked around and realized that one of the bags of food was gone. They've run away! Hugh thought. They came inside, and I was asleep, and they bolted.

He clenched his fists, then banged them on the table. How could he have let this happen? How? He called Smokey stupid, but his nephew's mistakes were nothing compared to this.

He had to find the two girls. Fast. If Smokey found out that the kids escaped while Hugh was supposed to be watching them, he would never hear the end of it. And what if they got away? What if they made it to the main road, flagged down a passing motorist, and got help?

Although Smokey was confident that the Edgertons would follow the instructions not to call police, Hugh suspected that the cops had been called immediately. By now every newspaper and TV station in the country had probably broadcast the kidnapping story, along with photos of the two missing girls.

Drivers today all seemed to be talking on cell phones. If those kids made it to the road, the first car that came along would stop, and call 911, and report that the missing girls had been found. The sheriff would be here in minutes, and Hugh would be back behind bars.

If the cops got here before Smokey returned, Hugh would have no way to escape. Without a car, he'd have to run for it, but no matter where he hid, they'd sic the police dogs on him. He couldn't even defend himself; the gun was in the car with Smokey.

He should have insisted that Smokey leave the gun at the cabin.

The girls would follow the road, Hugh decided. It was much faster than trying to cut through the woods, and Amy would want to get as much of a head start as possible.

Hugh took a swig of water, then rushed down the lane, running as fast as he could. I'll catch them, he told himself. I'll catch them before Smokey gets back, and when I do, they'll wish they had stayed put.

Up until now, Hugh had planned to release both girls. After they left Kendra where she'd be found quickly, he intended to take Amy to Oregon with them and drop her there. Or they could leave her tied up here in the cabin. If they did that, he knew it would be a while before she'd either be found or could get loose, and by then he and Smokey would be on a plane to New York, where they planned to get lost in the crowds of people. They already had the plane tickets, under assumed names, leaving Portland next Wednesday. They had their fake IDs, too. Hugh had taken care of that himself, not trusting Smokey to do it properly.

Now, as Hugh thought through those plans, he realized they needed to get rid of Amy before they let Kendra go. The girl was too smart, knew too much. He was pretty sure she had been looking at the license plate this morning, even though she had denied it, and now she had seized the first opportunity to try to escape.

Hugh used his sleeve to wipe sweat from his face.

When he got into this scheme, he had been determined to do nothing except help keep the little girl quiet while Smokey drove, and to stay with her while Smokey delivered the DVDs to Darielle.

Hugh had spent six months in prison for theft and assault, and he did not plan to ever serve another day.

It was hard to go straight, though. Employers were not eager to give an ex-con a second chance, and rents were high. He'd been out for over a month and was seriously short of cash. Smokey's kidnapping plan had offered a way out, an opportunity to start over. Hugh planned to commit only this one crime; then he'd have enough money to live on while he looked for work.

Of course, when he had agreed to help Smokey, the nanny was still in the picture. Darielle was going to stock her uncle's cabin with food for them, and she had agreed to meet Smokey halfway between that little store and her home to get each day's DVD, which she would sneak in to the Edgertons' house and leave where it would quickly be found.

Except for meeting Darielle, Smokey was supposed to stay at the cabin with Hugh. Instead, Smokey was driving around who knows where buying supplies and mailing the DVDs.

When the kid screamed so loud over the dropped toy that they had to return to the Edgerton house, Hugh had still thought they could pull off the kidnapping. He had not anticipated a young babysitter seeing them. He had certainly not counted on having to kidnap TWO kids.

Hugh's anger boiled as he hurried down the gravel road. He was angry at Darielle for breaking up with Smokey; he was angry at Smokey for not telling him, and for not having the sense to adjust their plans when his girlfriend backed out.

Most of all, he was angry at Amy for making a fool of him by running away.

Smokey intended to use his gun on Amy, and Hugh would not

stop him. When it was time to collect the money and go, they would leave Amy behind—but she would not be able to talk to the cops.

She would not talk, period, ever again.

Chapter Ten

Amy carried Kendra as long as she could, but eventually she had to let Kendra walk again. If she didn't put Kendra down, she was pretty sure her own arms were going to fall off. How could such a little kid be so heavy?

Amy looked at her watch. It was almost an hour since they had left the cabin. She didn't feel that they'd made much progress. She wished she'd brought more water. What she had was not going to last long enough.

Amy didn't see how it was possible for Kendra to poke along so slowly, but the child walked as if she had glue on the soles of her shoes.

"I'm going to run ahead and hide," Amy said. "Then you come and find me." Amy sprinted about twenty feet ahead, then crouched behind a bush. She knew she was in plain sight and expected Kendra to run forward to "find" her. Instead, the toddler sat down and started to cry.

Amy hurried back. "What's wrong?" she asked.

"Tubby go night-night."

It's time for her nap, Amy realized. She's never going to hustle along until she gets some sleep.

"We'll find a good spot to rest," Amy said. She picked up Kendra again, and carried her off the road into the woods. About twenty yards in, she came to a small clearing. The sun had warmed the wild grasses, and the clearing wasn't visible from the road. Perfect.

"You and Tubby can lie here in this nice warm grass," Amy said. Kendra plopped down.

"Tubby want blankee."

"I'm sorry I don't have a blanket. You'll have to close your eyes and pretend it's here."

Kendra closed her eyes and put her thumb in her mouth. Soon Amy could tell the little girl was asleep.

Amy was far too wound up to rest. She felt jumpy as she listened for any sounds from the road. Looking around at the clearing, she decided that while Kendra slept, she would search for sticks or rocks that she could make into a signal. This clearing was big enough to be seen if a plane happened to fly over.

Amy walked around the perimeter of the clearing, gathering branches. Some had already fallen; others she broke off trees. When her arms were full, she carried the branches to the center of the clearing.

She had watched a TV report once about a mountain climber who got caught in an avalanche. He had made a big *X* in the snow with his feet, and someone flying a small airplane had seen it. The pilot said that in the wilderness, anything that was made by a person would catch his attention.

Amy decided instead of an *X* she would form an arrow, with the tip of the arrow pointing toward the cabin. That would be as good as a sign reading THIS WAY.

First she tamped the grass down with her feet, stomping out the shape of the arrow.

Then she began laying the sticks down in a row until she had an arrow eight feet long, with the angled sides about three feet each. Kendra was still asleep, so Amy gathered more sticks and made it a double row so it would be even more visible from the air.

When the arrow was finished, Amy picked up the sleeping

Kendra, who protested groggily at being awakened. "We have to go," Amy said. As it was, they had spent much too long at the clearing.

They were not quite back to the road when she heard an engine coming toward them.

"Be quiet," she whispered as she clutched Kendra close. "We're going to hide." She was afraid to run, fearful that the movement would catch Smokey's eye. She dropped to the ground and knelt beside a fallen tree.

"Shh," she said. "Hold still."

"Tubby go potty," Kendra said.

"Not now. You'll have to wait. Shhh."

The engine sound was closer now; she heard the crunch of the gravel under the vehicle's tires.

I need to look, Amy thought. I need to peek just enough to be sure it's Smokey, because if it isn't, whoever it is could rescue us. Cautiously, she raised her head and peered through the tree branches. The noise grew louder. Then there was a blur of white as the van sped past.

Panic set in. The van would return long before she and Kendra could make it to the main road. They had to hide. But where? She thought of trying to climb one of the big trees, but she knew she'd never be able to get Kendra up, too.

Maybe she could use branches and leaves as camouflage. She would cover Kendra first, and then cover herself, and hope they would both go undetected. If the men looked in this area and didn't see the girls, they'd go on. They wouldn't come back to look here again.

"You get to have some more nap," Amy said. She had Kendra lie next to the trunk of a big pine tree, one whose branches swept almost to the ground. "I'm going to make you a blanket," Amy said. She found a couple of large pine branches and laid those on top of Kendra.

"Lie still and be quiet," Amy said. "I'm going to lie next to you and take a nap, too."

With her shoe, Amy scuffed some rotting leaves into a pile, then scooped them up and put them on Kendra's legs.

She worked fast, knowing she had little time. As she piled more branches next to Kendra, intending to pull them on top of herself as soon as she lay down, she heard the blare of the van's horn. Amy froze, listening. Next she heard voices shouting.

They were much closer than the cabin was. Hugh must already have been coming after her, and Smokey had found him on the road. She couldn't quite make out the words, but the angry tone was evident.

She stretched out beside Kendra and pulled the leaves and branches on top of herself. She didn't have much hope that her plan would work, but she didn't know what else to do. As she pulled a pine branch across her face, she heard the van door slam.

Smokey must have gotten out. If Hugh had already come that far down the road, she expected that they would begin looking from that point on.

But what if they returned to the cabin and searched there first? Maybe the door she'd heard was Hugh getting in the van. What if they didn't come back this way for an hour or more? Then instead of lying here in the dirt with branches on top of them, she and Kendra ought to be running as fast as they could toward the main road.

She listened carefully. Had they returned to the cabin or were they searching nearby?

Beside her, Kendra squirmed. Amy slid her hand over and patted Kendra, trying to keep her still.

"Tubby go potty," Kendra said.

Amy didn't see how it could be too critical, since Kendra had gone right before her nap. Maybe Kendra liked the novelty of going outside, and using a leaf to wipe herself.

"Soon," she whispered. "Right now we have to be extra quiet. Don't move. Tell Tubby not to move."

"Tubby want Mommy."

So do I, Amy thought. So do I.

She moved slightly, trying to get comfortable. She must be lying on small rocks or pinecones, but she didn't dare sit up and remove them. The pine needles scratched her cheeks; she inhaled their scent.

She heard Hugh say, "I'll look on this side of the road; you take that side."

Amy tried to stay calm. They were close. Much too close.

Then she heard Hugh's voice again: "Leave the gun in the car."

"Maybe I'll use it on Amy now."

"No. Not until we have the money."

"I might need it. What if we see a bear?"

Amy couldn't hear Hugh's response.

The van door slammed.

Amy heard twigs snapping as one of the men walked toward her in the woods. She didn't dare remind Kendra to be quiet; she could only hope that the child would think they were playing hide-and-seek, and would lie still and say nothing.

The footsteps passed. They sounded about twenty feet away, although Amy couldn't be sure.

"Hey!" Amy tensed at the sound of Smokey's shout.

"Come here, and look at this! They were here. They made a signal with sticks!"

She heard crashing through the woods, and knew Hugh was

joining Smokey. "It's an arrow," Hugh said. "It points toward the cabin."

"Yeah," Smokey said. "That's what it is."

"Smart kid," Hugh said. "Too smart."

She heard a lot of commotion then, and knew that the two men were destroying her arrow. They must be kicking the sticks into disarray, or throwing them back to the edges of the clearing.

"What if some pilot already saw this?" Smokey asked.

"Nobody saw it," Hugh said. "I've been here the whole time and there haven't been any planes flying around."

"One might have flown over while you were asleep," Smokey said.

"I wasn't sleeping," Hugh said. "I told you, the kids ran off while I was in the outhouse."

"Right."

The footsteps came closer.

"If they took time to pick up all those sticks and make an arrow," Hugh said, "they can't be far ahead of us."

Amy blinked back tears. It had been such a good idea, but no one flying over would see her arrow now. Instead of making a signal, she should have used that time to keep going, no matter how tired Kendra was.

The men continued to tromp through the underbrush, gradually moving farther away. Amy wondered how far they would go before they returned to the van. Although she and Kendra had escaped notice this time, they were now between the men and the van. She didn't see how they would dare to move until the men got back in the van and drove away. When would that be? How long would they search this part of the woods?

"Tubby hungwy," Kendra said.

Amy reached over and clamped her hand on the toddler's mouth. "Shh," she whispered.

Kendra rolled her head back and forth, and began to whimper.

Amy removed her hand. "Just a little longer," she whispered. "We have to be quiet."

She slid her hand down carefully, feeling for the plastic bag that hung on her belt.

Trying not to make any noise, she slipped her hand into the bag and found the package of beef jerky. It had not yet been opened, and Amy couldn't tear it with one hand. She felt for the remaining Hershey bar. She put her finger under the outer wrapper and ripped it, then opened the inner wrapper and broke off a piece of chocolate.

She could hear the rustle of paper and feel the movement of the camouflage that covered her, but she thought the men were too far away to notice. She eased her hand back up, and, staying under the branches, put a small piece of chocolate on Kendra's lips. Kendra opened her mouth and ate the candy.

The branches scratched Amy's bare arms. She wanted to rub them, but she didn't dare. She felt dirty, and itchy, and scared.

The smell of the sweet chocolate mingled with the scent of the fir branches. Amy was hungry, too, but she decided to save the candy bar for Kendra.

Some diet, Amy thought. Kendra needs protein and veggies and a kiddie vitamin and instead I feed her a chocolate bar. But it worked to keep her quiet and right now that was all that mattered. Kendra could have nutritious meals later, after they got rescued. *If* they got rescued.

She continued to break off small pieces of chocolate and feed them to Kendra.

Eventually, she heard the van's engine start, followed by the sound of tires on gravel. The noise went toward the cabin. She was surprised that they had given up the search so quickly. Maybe they were going to get something to eat.

Amy waited, listening. The car noise faded until she could no longer hear it. She took a deep breath, then sat up.

"You can go potty now," she said as she brushed the branches and leaves off Kendra.

When that was accomplished, they each had a drink of water. Amy opened the bag of beef jerky, to eat as they walked.

Amy took Kendra's hand and led her back to the road. "We have to hurry," she said, "and be quiet."

The road ahead curved through the trees, and Amy walked quickly toward the curve. As she came around the bend, she saw a figure ahead.

Hugh sat on the side of the road, waiting.

Chapter Eleven

Amy stopped.

"Well, well," Hugh said. "Look who's here." He stood up, stretched, and strolled toward the girls.

Amy knew it was useless to run. Kendra was too slow on her own, and too heavy for Amy to carry. They would never get away. She stood still, and watched Hugh approach.

"I figured you had to be close by," Hugh said. "How far could you get with the kid in tow? It seemed easier to sit here and wait for you to come to me than to wear myself out searching for you."

Amy said nothing. She felt as if a plug had been pulled, and all of her determination and hope were leaking out.

"You shouldn't have tried to get away," Hugh said. "You only made Smokey angry."

"He's always angry," she said.

"He had a rough childhood. His dad died when he was ten, and he never had enough money."

"That's no excuse to be a criminal," Amy said. "My dad died, too, and my mom needs money, but I'm not going to steal cars and kidnap children."

Hugh looked startled. "Your dad died? How?"

"He was in a car accident. That's why I do babysitting, to help out."

Tears brimmed in Amy's eyes. It wasn't fair! Smokey and

Hugh, who spent their days stealing, lying, and kidnapping, were still here, while her dad, who worked hard and was kind and honest, got killed.

Hugh nodded toward the cabin. "Let's go home," he said. "Smokey's waiting."

Now what? Amy wondered as she trudged back to the cabin. She knew there wouldn't be another opportunity to escape; Hugh and Smokey would be vigilant about watching her from now on.

Even if she got another chance to run, Amy didn't want to try again. It was too hard, with Kendra. Alone, Amy could have run much farther, maybe all the way to the big road, before the van returned.

She blinked back tears, knowing she would never try to escape alone, even if she had the chance. She would stay with Kendra and try to protect her.

Smokey was outside when they approached.

"I found them," Hugh called.

"Where were they?"

"Walking down the road, like I thought would happen."

"How long was Hugh asleep before you took off?" Smokey asked Amy.

Amy looked at the two men. Smokey sneered at Hugh. A vein in Hugh's temple throbbed.

"He wasn't asleep," Amy said. "We left while he was in the bathroom."

She saw the surprise and relief in Hugh's eyes. She wasn't sure why she had lied to Smokey, except that Hugh was not as eager to hurt her as Smokey was, and she wanted to keep it that way. If she could stay on the good side of Hugh, maybe he would decide to let her live when they released Kendra.

Or maybe not.

Smokey stepped toward Amy. "I need to teach Miss Smarty-pants a lesson," he said. "Let her know what happens when she doesn't do what we say."

"No," said Hugh.

"You can't just let her get away with this," Smokey said.

"She didn't get away with anything. She's here, isn't she? They both are. If you send a film that shows the girl all beat up, the Edgertons might get mad and not pay the ransom."

"I wouldn't have to put her in the film next time."

Amy held her breath. If Smokey didn't put her in the video, she wouldn't be able to give the signal and send the nanny clue.

"She won't run away again," Hugh said. "Will you?" he asked Amy.

She shook her head. Right then she was so weary, she wouldn't have been able to run three feet.

"Tubby hungwy," Kendra said.

"We're all hungry," Hugh said. He walked to the table, where Smokey had set the new bags of groceries, and began pulling out Smokey's purchases.

When Amy saw the hot dogs and buns, her mouth watered. "Can we roast hot dogs?" she asked.

"Tubby like hot dog," Kendra said.

Hugh pulled the coffee out of the grocery bag. "You doofus!" he said. "You bought whole coffee beans. How am I supposed to grind coffee beans?"

"You said you wanted coffee; I bought coffee," Smokey said.

"I have a caffeine-withdrawal headache that won't quit, and you bring me whole coffee beans," Hugh said.

Smokey brought some kindling and two logs inside and began laying the fire.

"We'll look for long sticks," Amy said. She took Kendra's hand and walked outside.

"Keep on eye on them," Smokey said.

Hugh followed the girls out.

It wasn't hard to find sticks that would work, and soon the hot dogs were roasting over the fire.

Amy threaded the buns on an extra stick and toasted them.

She slid a sizzling hot dog into a bun for Kendra. "Let it cool a minute," she warned.

"Tubby want catch-up," Kendra said.

"Any mustard?" Hugh asked.

Amy was tempted to ask for relish but decided not to when she saw the dark cloud on Smokey's face.

"You don't like what I buy," Smokey said, "you can go yourself next time. I'll stay with the kids tomorrow."

Amy tensed, hoping Hugh would not agree to do that. The last thing she wanted was to be left in the cabin with Smokey while Hugh drove to town.

After they ate, Amy practiced the animal-sound game with Kendra once more before Smokey decided to make the second DVD.

When he began filming, Amy said, "Kendra and I have a new game that we're going to show you. She and Tubby have learned some animal sounds."

"Tubby say meow, meow," Kendra said.

"That's right. The baby cat says meow, meow. What does the daddy dog say?"

"Woof. Woof."

"Right," Amy said. "What does the baby chicken say?"

"Peep. Peep."

"Good! What does the daddy donkey say?"

As always, Kendra got excited about the donkey. "Heehaw!" she yelled. "Heehaw! Heehaw!"

"Good," Amy said.

Amy scratched her right ear.

"Donkey say heehaw!" Kendra cried.

Quickly Amy scratched her left ear. "What does the mama goat say?" she asked.

"Donkey say heehaw!"

Amy rubbed both ears again. "The mama goat," she said. "What does the mama goat say?"

"Naaa," said Kendra. "Naaa."

"Right!" Amy felt such relief that she had been able to give the signal, and slip the mama-goat clue in, that she had trouble remembering what other animal sounds she had taught Kendra. She paused, trying to gather her wits.

Kendra jumped up and began running in circles. "Heehaw!" she shouted. "Heehaw!"

"Cut!" yelled Smokey.

"Heehaw!"

"No more of that game," Hugh said. "She gets too excited."

That was okay with Amy. The whole purpose of the animal sound game had been to let the police know they should talk to Kendra's nanny. She had done that.

Kendra shrieked, "Baby cat heehaw. Daddy dog heehaw!"

Either she's on a sugar high from all the chocolate, Amy thought, or she's overtired, or both.

"I'm going to tell Tubby a story," Amy said. She sat down under the window. "Come here, Tubby."

Kendra stopped running.

"Once upon a time," Amy said, "there was a little striped gray cat named Tubby who liked to go swimming."

Kendra walked over to Amy and sat beside her.

"Tubby always wore a life jacket," Amy said. She continued, keeping her voice low, and before long, Kendra had put her head in Amy's lap, and was sound asleep.

Hugh and Smokey replayed the second video, then Smokey put it in an envelope, and added postage. "All set to mail tomorrow morning," he said.

By then, Amy thought, the police will have seen the first DVD. They could be searching the state for a white Caravan.

DAY THREE

Chapter Twelve

Jorja stayed at Amy's house the second night, too, so she was there when the police officer came on Wednesday morning.

"Have you found them?" Mrs. Nordlund asked, when she opened the door and saw Detective Rockport.

"No, but the kidnapper mailed a DVD to the Edgertons. I brought a copy for you to watch. Do you have a DVD player?"

"Yes."

"The package was postmarked Olympia, so we know that they went south."

As Mrs. Nordlund, Jorja, and Detective Rockport watched the video, Jorja stared at Amy, wondering how this could be happening. How could her best friend be missing? Who had made this DVD? Where was Amy?

When it got to the part about Aunt Cara and Uncle Van, Mrs. Nordlund said, "Wait a minute." The officer hit *pause*. "Amy doesn't have an Aunt Cara or an Uncle Van," she said.

"It's a clue!" Jorja said. "She's trying to tell us something!"

Detective Rockport played that part again. This time it continued, and Amy said, "And also Mrs. White."

"I don't know a Mrs. White, either," Mrs. Nordlund said. She turned to Jorja. "Do you? Is there someone at school named Mrs. White? A teacher? Does Amy have a friend whose mother is Mrs. White?"

Jorja shook her head. "I don't know anyone named White," she said.

"Maybe when this video gets played on TV," Mrs. Nordlund said, "someone will recognize the background. It looks like an old house. There might be some distinctive mark."

"We won't be releasing this to the media," Detective Rockport said.

"But don't you want as many people as possible to see it? It would help them recognize Amy and Kendra."

"I think Jorja's correct," Detective Rockport replied. "By talking about people who don't exist, Amy is trying to send us information. The kidnapper obviously didn't catch on, but it would be easy for some investigative reporter to discover that there is no Aunt Cara or Uncle Van, and make a big deal out of it. I can almost hear the news clips: 'Kidnapped Girl Sends Clues to Cops.' The kidnapper is probably watching the news reports and reading the papers. It wouldn't be good if he or she knows Amy is trying to outsmart him."

"Cara. Van. White," Jorja said.

"I think she's telling us what kind of vehicle to look for," the officer said.

"Of course!" Mrs. Nordlund said. "A white Caravan!"

Detective Rockport nodded. "That's right."

Goose bumps rose on Jorja's arms. Amy had thought of a way to let the police know what kind of vehicle the kidnapper had! How smart was that? Jorja wanted to holler, "You go, girl!" and give Amy a big high five.

They watched the video two more times but didn't notice anything else that might be useful.

"You'll need to keep this information to yourself," Detective Rockport warned. "It's crucial that nobody else finds out that

Amy sent a message. If we can keep this secret so that the kidnapper doesn't figure out what Amy is doing, she may send another clue in the next DVD."

"I won't tell anyone," Jorja promised.

"If the public knew about the white Caravan," Mrs. Nordlund said, "you'd probably get lots of tips. One might lead you to Amy and Kendra."

"There are many white Caravans on the road. We'll be looking for those, of course, but we need more than that to go on. If the kidnapper knows that we've been alerted to the white Caravan, he won't let Amy be in the videos anymore. Or he might switch to a different vehicle. It's important that he not catch on, in case she's able to send other clues."

Mrs. Nordlund frowned.

"It's also safer for Amy," the officer said.

Mrs. Nordlund sighed. "All right," she said. "I won't tell."

"I'll let you know if we learn anything else," he said.

After he left, Mrs. Nordlund said, "She seemed okay, didn't she? She didn't look as if they had hurt her."

"She looked fine," Jorja said, "and so did Kendra."

"I wonder if she got a bug bite," Mrs. Nordlund said. "She was scratching at the side of her head."

Minutes later, Detective Rockport sent out an alert to every law enforcement agency in the state, to be on the lookout for a white Dodge Caravan in connection with the kidnapping of the two girls. He also alerted the FBI, who were acting as consultants on the high-profile case.

Half an hour later, another message was posted. A white Dodge Caravan had been reported stolen in West Seattle on Monday. The owner had left the keys in it while she picked up an order at Husky's Deli, and when she returned, her van was gone.

Detective Rockport released the license-plate number to the media with a story about the woman. She had been getting fruit trays and sandwiches for the reception following her mother's funeral when her car got stolen. The story generated a lot of sympathy and the license-plate number was broadcast on all the local channels.

Sometimes you get lucky, Detective Rockport thought. While it might not be the van the kidnapper used, chances were good that it was. The timing was perfect. Now, instead of a vague description, the public had a specific license-plate number to look for, and by using the funeral story, it wasn't necessary to connect the van to the kidnapping in order to create interest.

Maybe they'd get lucky again, and the van would be spotted. Detective Rockport hoped so. He had a daughter himself. The thought of her being kidnapped turned his stomach. He couldn't imagine how terrible this was for Amy's mom and Kendra's parents.

Mrs. Nordlund had clearly wanted the video to be broadcast, in the hope that a stranger would recognize the location. He decided to return to her house, and tell her about the stolen-car report. That would make her feel better about keeping the video secret.

The men gave Amy no more opportunities to escape. Except for when she was actually inside the outhouse, one of them watched her constantly. If she took Kendra for a walk, Hugh or Smokey trailed them. When she pumped water and washed Kendra's face, one of the men observed.

It didn't matter. Amy would not have tried to run away again even if she had the chance. With Kendra dawdling along, running away was too hard.

She needed to come up with the next clue. The Saddle Stop Country Store would be a great clue if she could figure out how to do it. Unlike a Safeway or a Kroger's, it was such a distinctive name that there wouldn't be any others. If she could let the police know the name of the store, it would lead them to this area.

There was no way she could actually say the words *Saddle Stop Country Store* while Smokey was filming her without Hugh and Smokey hearing it. They'd delete that, for sure.

Amy and her friends sometimes played charades, where one person wordlessly acted out a book or song title or the name of a movie, while the others tried to guess. The signal for "sounds like" was to tug on an earlobe. She remembered once when Jorja was acting out "The Three Little Pigs" and she kept pulling on her earlobe and then pretending to dig a hole, trying to get her friends to say, "digs." Eventually, someone did and then the "sounds like" signal led them to "pigs."

Amy decided to think of words that sounded like *saddle*, *stop*, *country*, and *store*. She would make the "sounds like" gesture, then say those words, and hope that someone watching would figure it out. She didn't have to depend only on Jorja for this clue. Lots of people played charades. Plenty of people might recognize the "sounds like" signal.

First Amy thought of words that sounded like *saddle*. *Rattle, paddle, straddle, fiddle-faddle, skedaddle.* She wished she had her rhyming dictionary, which she used when she wrote poetry. Even without it, she had a long mental list of possible words.

As a writer, Amy loved words and it was fun to think of as many as possible that sounded like *saddle*.

Stop was even easier. Lots of words rhyme with *stop*. *Chop, crop, drop, flip-flop, hop, top, mop, pop, swap.* She had a dozen words in seconds.

Country was a problem. Try as she might, Amy couldn't come up with a single word that rhymed with *country*. Finally she decided to skip *country*, and go on to *store*. If she sent clues for *Saddle Stop Store*, and if the police figured out those clues, that ought to be close enough to bring them to the right place.

Store, Amy thought. *Bore, lore, floor, core, chore, door.* She was on a roll now: *pour, roar, swore, tore.*

Even with so many good words to choose from, she worried about the "sounds like" clue. The gesture of pulling on an earlobe was so close to the ear scratching that had been her signal in the previous DVDs that Amy wasn't sure anyone would catch on.

The ear-scratch signal had required both ears and it was a scratching motion, whereas the "sounds like" signal was a tug on only one earlobe, but both signals involved the ears and Amy knew it might get confusing. Still, she had to try. She couldn't think of a better way to transmit the necessary information.

With any luck, by now the police were looking for a white Caravan, and as soon as they saw the second DVD, Amy hoped they would interview Kendra's nanny. The nanny knows where the cabin is. She could lead the police here!

Maybe the nanny was traveling in Europe and nobody knew how to reach her. Or what if she lied and pretended not to know anything about the kidnapping? What if she decided to wait for her share of the ransom? Maybe she was scared of Smokey and what he might do if she told the police what she knew.

Amy had trouble concentrating on potential clues because Kendra kept interrupting, and distracting her. I need a pencil and paper, Amy thought, to keep all of this straight.

But even if she had pencil and paper, she knew she couldn't write the clues down. She didn't want Hugh or Smokey to know what she was doing. She had to keep everything clear in her mind.

She had to find words that rhymed, figure out how to relay the message, and amuse Kendra, all at the same time.

"We're going to learn a new game," Amy announced. "We're going to pretend that you and Tubby have a boat, and you're going to paddle the boat and give Tubby a ride."

"Tubby like boat," Kendra said.

"Good. Do you know what a paddle is? To make the boat go?"

Kendra shook her head, no.

Amy picked up a paper plate. "This can be your paddle," she said. "It works like this." Holding the plate in both hands, Amy made a swooping motion beside her, as if she were in a canoe, dipping the plate in and out of a stream. "I'm pretending my boat is in the water," she said, "and when I push my paddle through the water, it makes the boat go." She paddled with the plate for a few seconds, first on one side, then the other, while she moved around the room.

"Now you do it." She handed the plate to Kendra. Kendra held Tubby in one hand, and the plate in the other.

Amy said, "Paddle."

Kendra paddled furiously, her arm rotating like a windmill.

"Good!" Amy said. "You're making the boat go. Paddle!"

Kendra began walking around while she whirled her arm.

"When I tell you to stop," Amy said, "you need to quit. Then we'll go again."

"Tubby like boat," Kendra said, swooping both arms around, and starting to run.

"Stop!" Amy said.

Kendra paused briefly, then said, "Tubby make boat go."

"Paddle!" Amy said.

Kendra swept her arms around.

"Door," Amy said. "Paddle your boat to the door."

"Tubby go boat!" yelled Kendra as she flailed her arms in giant circles and raced around the cabin.

"Knock it off," said Smokey.

"Stop," said Amy.

Kendra kept running.

"Stop!" said Amy.

Kendra shouted, "Boat say heehaw!" She kept running, paddling furiously.

"I said, knock it off!" Smokey took a step toward Kendra.

Quickly, Amy grabbed Kendra's arm. "We're going to play a different game now. Come and sit by me."

Kendra struggled briefly, then collapsed beside Amy.

Amy decided one rehearsal with the paddle was enough. She hoped when it came time to make the next DVD, Kendra wouldn't get so wild that Smokey called a halt before Amy had given all the clues.

Mentally, she went through it again. *Paddle. Stop. Door.* She would give the "sounds like" signal before she said "paddle," and again before she said "door." Even though she had so many words that rhymed with *stop*, it seemed better to use the real word *stop* than to try to add a third "sounds like."

She had no idea if anyone would catch on this time. All she could do was try.

Chapter Thirteen

That night, Amy lay awake long after Kendra, Hugh, and Smokey fell asleep. Although she kept her eyes open, she saw nothing. Her room at home had always seemed dark during the night, but it was a lighted stage compared to the cabin. With no streetlights outside the window, no neighbors, and no headlights from passing traffic, the forest was completely dark.

Inside there were no digital clocks nor any of the small lights that glow on various electronic devices such as the cordless phone or the base of the electric toothbrush. Total blackness filled the cabin.

She wondered what her mom was doing. She imagined her watching the DVD that Smokey had made. Amy was confident that, even without her signal, Mom would pick up on the first clue and tell the police that Amy had no Aunt Cara and Uncle Van. She would tell them there's no Mrs. White, either.

By now Amy was sure that the police were searching for a white Caravan, but they didn't know where to look. She didn't know how many white Caravans were being driven in the state of Washington, but she was fairly sure there were a lot of them.

The nanny clue was good only if Kendra's nanny cooperated. If she was the kind of person who got involved in a plot to kidnap her employer's child, she could not be counted on to be honest. Even if the police interviewed her, the nanny might lie. She might be scared of getting arrested, or, as Smokey said, afraid of what he would do to her if she told the police about the plan.

I have to do more to save us, Amy thought. The clues may or may not work. Tomorrow is already our fourth day. Hugh acted more nervous each day, and Smokey was increasingly antagonistic. Kendra, who had been such an angel at first, was having cranky spells and had cried for her mother that night, before she fell asleep.

We're all on edge, Amy thought, and that isn't good. She worried most about Smokey and what he might do. She wished he didn't have a gun.

That's when the idea struck her. *Maybe I can get the gun.* Hugh had told Smokey to leave the gun in the glove compartment of the van. What if she could sneak out of the cabin while both men were sleeping, and take the gun?

Even in the dark, she was sure she could find the van. She knew where it was parked. Was it locked? She didn't think so. There was no need to lock it way out here. She wasn't positive the van was unlocked, but there was a greater risk of waking one of the men if she tried to find the keys and take them than if she simply left the cabin.

She decided to take a chance that the car was not locked. She rolled out from under the blanket that she shared with Kendra, and stood up. Smokey's even breathing and Hugh's snoring continued.

She felt on the floor for her shoes, then put them on.

Amy took small steps, moving her feet slowly to be sure she didn't trip on anything. She held her hands out in front of her, feeling for the edge of the table.

When she got to it, her hand closed around the flashlight that lay on top. It would be faster to find the gun if she took the flashlight. But last night, she'd heard Hugh get up in the night and go outside, presumably to use the bathroom. What if that happened again while she was out of the cabin? If the flashlight wasn't on the table where it was supposed to be, he would know someone else had it, and she would be caught.

She decided it was better to go in the dark. Leaving the flashlight on the table, she slowly made her way past the sleeping men to the cabin door.

She turned the knob carefully, then pushed the door open and stepped outside. She closed the door behind her, trying to avoid the slight *click* sound by releasing the knob slowly.

Overhead, the stars glittered. Against the black blanket of sky, they seemed brighter and bigger than at home. Off to her right, an owl hooted softly, high in a tree.

Amy wanted to hurry, but she was afraid of tripping and falling, so she moved slowly toward the passenger side of the van. She pressed her forehead against the side window, trying to see whether or not the lock was pushed down. In the dim light, she couldn't tell.

Amy grasped the door handle, imagining the loud *beep beep beep* sound that would fill the forest if the car was locked and she triggered the alarm. She shivered, then pulled on the handle. The door slid soundlessly open. As it did, the interior light came on. Squinting at the sudden light, Amy quickly sat in the van and pulled the door closed. The light stayed on. Amy realized it must automatically stay on for a short time. She hoped the delay would be brief. If one of the men saw a light out here, she'd be a goner.

After several seconds, the light went off. Amy sat still, trying to calm her nerves and letting her eyes readjust to the dark. She needed to be careful when she took the gun out of the glove compartment. She didn't want to accidentally pull the trigger.

There were no guns in her home. Her dad had not hunted, nor did her mom. Amy had never used a gun, had never even held one in her hand. She didn't plan to use one now; she only wanted to be sure that it wasn't used on her.

She would take Smokey's gun and bury it in the woods where he'd never find it. Doing so might save her own life.

If Smokey had the gun, it would be easy to shoot her; without the gun, getting rid of her would be more complicated. By the time the men discovered the gun was missing, she hoped they would be in a hurry to get out of town, and would end up leaving her at the cabin.

Amy took a deep breath, then lifted the latch, opening the glove compartment. She stuck her hand inside, feeling for the gun.

It wasn't there.

She groped the whole inside of the glove compartment but found only a folded paper that felt like a map, and a plastic scraper, to take ice off the windshield.

What had Smokey done with the gun? Had he hidden it somewhere else to be sure that Hugh didn't get it? Was he carrying it with him all the time, even though Hugh had asked him not to?

As she sat there, wondering where else to look, a light appeared at the door of the cabin. One of the men was coming out with the flashlight! Had they realized she was gone? Were they looking for her?

Amy slumped in the seat, watching. Hugh's face appeared ghostlike in the faint glow behind the flashlight. If he had come out two minutes earlier, he would have seen the car light go on when she opened the door.

The flashlight moved straight from the cabin to the outhouse, then disappeared as Hugh went inside. A short time later, he emerged and headed back toward the cabin.

What if he shines it around the inside of the cabin before he turns it off? Amy thought. He would notice that I'm not there. He'll come looking for me.

Although she told herself he wouldn't shine the light around inside the cabin because he wouldn't want to wake up the others, she tensed as Hugh went back inside and closed the door.

She waited. If he was going to discover that she was gone, it would happen right now.

The car smelled of stale cigarette smoke. Outside, a slight breeze rustled the leaves on the trees. The cabin remained dark, and silent. He had not noticed her absence.

She wondered if Smokey might have hidden the gun somewhere else in the car—under one of the floor mats, perhaps, or in the back. As long as she was here, she decided to search the car thoroughly.

She ran her hands across the floor and tried to reach under the seat, but there was a locked storage cubby. She leaned over to the driver's side and felt under that seat. As she straightened up, her elbow hit the steering column and she heard a jingling sound. Was that keys?

Quickly she ran her hands across the side of the steering column and found the car keys dangling from the ignition. She had worried that the car would be locked; instead it was not only unlocked but the keys were in it.

If I knew how to drive, Amy thought, I could escape right now. I could start the van and drive to safety.

Smokey and Hugh could never catch her on foot. Even if Smokey had the gun with him, by the time they heard the car and realized what was happening, and ran outside, she would be out of range of his bullets.

She wondered if she could do it. She'd watched other people drive. All they did was turn the key, then shift into gear and step on the gas pedal. Shift, how? What if she started the car but couldn't figure out how to get it out of park and into drive? She ran her hands over the area around the steering wheel, feeling for the shift. This must be what it's like to be blind, she thought, to try to learn through your fingertips rather than your eyes.

Amy sat behind the wheel, then tried shifting. The gearshift didn't budge. She wondered if the engine had to be running in order to change gears. Should she turn it on? Should she try to leave?

What about Kendra? She imagined going back to get Kendra—waking her up and trying to keep her quiet while Amy carried her to the car. It would never work. Kendra was a darling when she was rested and well fed, but she was as fussy as any other three-year-old when she was hungry or tired. Waking her up to take her along would not be smart. If Amy took off in the car now, she'd have to leave Kendra behind.

Perhaps that was still the best thing to do. If Amy could drive the car, she should be able to find help within an hour. The Saddle Stop Country Store probably wasn't open at night but she might see another car. If not, she'd go straight down the road to the first town.

The police would rescue Kendra immediately. Maybe Hugh and Smokey wouldn't hear the engine start and wouldn't even know she was gone until the police arrived. Even if they did hear her drive off, and they took Kendra and ran, how far could they get before they were caught? The police would use helicopters and bloodhounds to track them.

On the other hand, a car can be dangerous, and she knew absolutely nothing about how to drive. What if she hit a tree or ran off the road into a ditch? What if she hit another car? She could kill herself, or someone else, by attempting to escape.

And then there was the unpredictability of Smokey. He would be irate if she drove away. Furious enough to take out his anger on Kendra? Angry enough to say if he can't have the ransom money, they can't have their child back alive?

She wished she could find the gun.

They had driven a long way that first night after they left town, before they turned in to the cabin's lane. She didn't want to drive that far. She didn't want to drive at all.

I'll save driving the car as my last chance, she decided. Now that she knew Smokey left the keys in it, she could race to the car any time, and try to use it to get away. She would wait a while longer, in case her clues worked and help arrived. If it didn't . . . well, she would make her driving debut then, if she had to.

She didn't want the light to come on until she was ready to go inside, so she climbed over the seat and felt for the gun on the floor by the middle seat.

The far backseat had cubbies on both sides. She found papers, a hairbrush, empty beverage cans, and two pencils—but no gun.

When she finished her search, she opened the car door and got out, quickly closing the door, then waiting until the light turned off. She quietly let herself into the cabin, and crawled back under the blanket beside Kendra.

Even though she had not found the gun, her trip to the van had been worthwhile. Now she knew that if she got desperate, she could jump in the car, lock the doors, and drive away. Or, at least, *try* to drive away.

She fell asleep wondering where Smokey had put the gun.

DAY FOUR

Chapter Fourteen

When the second DVD arrived, Detective Rockport hurried to the Edgerton home, and played it three times, trying to pick up any clue from Amy. Nothing struck him. Of course he realized she couldn't say anything obvious or the kidnapper would realize what she was doing.

"The postmark is Olympia again," Detective Rockport said, "so they are probably holed up somewhere."

"Have you alerted the police in Olympia?" Mr. Edgerton asked.

"Yes, but a package postmarked Olympia wasn't necessarily mailed there. Mail from small towns and rural areas is processed in the bigger cities."

This video showed her playing a word game with Kendra, a "What does the animal say?" game. The background was the same building as the first film.

Maybe there would be no more clues. Probably the girl had no idea where she was being held. She had tried to help—and had—when she provided the make of the car. Maybe that was the best she could do.

It bothered him that the white Caravan had not yet been found. Once they had the license-plate number, he had hoped the vehicle would be spotted, but that had not happened.

Wherever the kidnapper was holding those girls, he must have a garage or other storage facility, and was keeping the van out of sight.

It was painful to watch the Edgertons' distress when they saw the video of Kendra. Mrs. Edgerton cried through the whole thing. Mr. Edgerton struggled with his emotions, too.

"Kendra looks unhurt," Detective Rockport pointed out. "Amy seems to be doing a good job of entertaining her. Did you play the animal-sound game with Kendra, or is that something Amy taught her?"

"We never played it," Mrs. Edgerton said. "Kendra likes books with pictures of animals, but I never tried to teach her the noises."

"Maybe her nanny played it with her," Detective Rockport said.

"I doubt it," Mrs. Edgerton said. "Darielle relied on TV or toys rather than interactive games. That's one reason we were looking for someone to replace her."

"You planned to let her go?" Detective Rockport asked. "Did she know that?"

"No."

"Do you think Darielle might be involved in this?" Mr. Edgerton asked.

"I need to follow every possible angle."

"She didn't know we weren't satisfied," Mrs. Edgerton said. "She seemed fond of Kendra; I'm sure she wouldn't do anything to jeopardize her."

"Was there any other reason you were dissatisfied with her service?"

"She has been Kendra's nanny for only a couple of months," Mr. Edgerton said, "but she's already asked for a raise. That bothered me, since we pay a generous salary."

It bothered Detective Rockport, too. He had tried twice to contact Darielle at her home, but got voice mail both times. She had not returned his calls. Even on vacation, most people pick up their messages. He decided to stop at her apartment.

Before he did that, he went to Mrs. Nordlund's house to show the DVD to her. Amy's friend Jorja was there again and so were Mrs. Nordlund's parents. No one picked up anything unusual in what Amy said on the film.

"She's a good babysitter," Mrs. Nordlund said. "She's keeping little Kendra happy."

"Yes," Detective Rockport agreed, "she is."

"She still has the bug bites," Mrs. Nordlund said.

"What?" Detective Rockport said.

"She keeps scratching at her ears," Mrs. Nordlund said. "She did it in the first video, and she does it again here. Watch."

They replayed the DVD and watched as Amy scratched first her right ear and then her left ear.

"See that?" Mrs. Nordlund said. "It's as if her ears itch. I wonder if the place she's staying has fleas."

"Wait!" Jorja said. "I just thought of something!" She jumped up, ran to Amy's room, and came back with Amy's green notebook. She flipped through the pages of writing until she found the part she wanted.

"Here," she said, showing the story to Mrs. Nordlund and Detective Rockport. "I couldn't sleep last night, so I read a story that Amy is writing."

Detective Rockport looked where Jorja pointed, and began to read aloud: "'I'll scratch my ears, as a signal. First I'll scratch my right ear and then I'll scratch my left ear. Whatever I do next is the message.'"

Detective Rockport quit reading, and played the DVD again. When Amy scratched her right ear and then her left ear, he nodded. The next thing Amy said was, "What does the mama goat say?" When Kendra didn't respond right away, Amy scratched both ears again and repeated the question, "What does the mama goat say?" She was clearly emphasizing the words *mama goat*

He stopped the DVD player.

"That's a clue," Jorja said. "It has to be! She doesn't scratch her ears any other time."

"Let's look at the first DVD again," Mrs. Nordlund said. "I remember the scratching, but I don't recall when it happened."

They played the first DVD. Amy scratched her ears before she said, "Tell Aunt Cara and Uncle Van not to worry."

"She's giving us the signal, just like in her story," Jorja said. "The first time the clue was *white Caravan*. This time it's *mama goat*."

"*Mama goat*," Mrs. Nordlund said. "*Mama goat* doesn't mean anything to me."

Detective Rockport suddenly stood up. "It does to me," he said. "Good work, Jorja. I'll be in touch."

He left the Nordlund home, got in his car, and headed for Darielle Monroe's apartment. A mama goat is a nanny, he thought. Amy must be telling us that Kendra's nanny is involved in the kidnapping. This might be the break the case needed.

When Detective Rockport knocked at the door of Darielle's apartment, no one answered. He knocked on the apartment next to hers, but nobody responded there, either. He wrote *Please call. Urgent* on the back of a business card and slid it under Darielle's door.

Back in the apartment lobby, he looked at all the names on the mailboxes until he found the one that said *Manager* under the person's name. He went to that apartment number and knocked.

The door was opened by a harried-looking young woman carrying a crying baby. Behind her, Detective Rockport saw two more young children.

"Mrs. Burton?" he asked, handing her a business card.

"Yes. Is something wrong?"

"I'm trying to contact one of the tenants in this building,"

Detective Rockport said. "Darielle Monroe. She hasn't returned my calls."

"She isn't here," Mrs. Burton said.

"Do you know where she went?"

The woman shook her head no. "The only reason I even know she's away is that she left when I happened to be sweeping the front walk. She had a suitcase, and when I asked if she was taking a trip, she said, 'Yes, I'm going on vacation.'"

"Did she say where she was going?"

"I asked her that, and she said she was going to heaven."

"Heaven? You're sure that's what she said."

"It seemed odd to me, too, but she looked happy and excited, so I figured wherever she was going, it must seem like heaven to her."

"Did someone pick her up? Was she with anyone?"

"She took a Yellow Cab. I didn't see anyone in it except the driver."

"What day was this?"

"Monday afternoon. I'm sure, because I always sweep the walk on Mondays, after the garbage has been collected."

"Do you know if she has family in this area? Someone I could contact who might know how to reach her?"

"No. She's only lived here a couple of months, and she kept to herself. She has a job, or at least she leaves every morning at six-thirty and doesn't get home until about five. When she rented the apartment, she said she worked as a nanny."

The woman jiggled the fussy baby up and down. "She has a boyfriend, but I don't know his name. He is here sometimes on the weekends."

"Thanks for your help," Detective Rockport said. "If she comes home, I'd appreciate a call."

"Is Darielle in trouble?"

"I want to question her about a case involving someone she knows."

Detective Rockport returned to his car and called in a request for the department to find out where a Yellow Cab had gone last Monday after it picked up a fare at this address.

He wondered if Darielle was really on vacation or if her trip had something to do with Kendra's disappearance. The fact that Darielle had left town the same day as the kidnapping seemed like too much of a coincidence.

On the other hand, her conversation with the apartment manager sounded innocent enough. A young woman on her way to a dream destination might well say "heaven" when asked where she was going, whereas a woman on her way to commit a crime would likely act nervous.

Darielle rubbed more sunscreen on her legs, then lay back in her beach chair. This is what a vacation should be: total relaxation. No responsibilities, no telephone, no TV—just lying in the sun, eating when she was hungry, and going for a swim when she got too warm. Best of all, someone else was paying for everything.

She still could barely believe her good fortune. A week ago she was running after a spoiled three-year-old every day, and going out with a petty crook at night.

Now here she was in Honolulu while her new boyfriend attended a conference. He was gone all day, which was fine with Darielle, arriving back at the hotel in time to take her out for a leisurely dinner and maybe some dancing.

She slept late every morning, then headed straight to the beach. What a life!

She thought back to the night she had met Jeff. She had been standing on the corner in the rain, waiting for Smokey to pick her up. Smokey was late, as usual. Jeff came along, hailed a cab, then asked Darielle if his cab could drop her somewhere. By then, she was so disgusted with Smokey that she said, "Why not?" and climbed in.

She ended up having dinner with Jeff, and he called her again the next day. Two days later, she broke up with Smokey, telling him not to call her again.

Looking back, she wondered why she had ever let herself get involved with a loser like Smokey in the first place. He was all talk and no action—full of big schemes for getting rich, none of which he ever followed through on.

Jeff, on the other hand, was already rich, and as far as Darielle was concerned, that was the most important attribute any man could have. She didn't care if he was honest, or kind, or smart or interesting, but she cared if he had money.

Smokey had lied to her in the beginning, telling her he was getting a big inheritance from his grandparents, but the inheritance never happened and she later found out Smokey's grandparents were still living. She should have dumped him then.

Well, he was out of her life now and good riddance. Darielle hoped she never saw him again.

"Let's get started on the next film," Smokey said. He turned to Amy. "What are you going to say this time?"

"We're going to play the boat game," Amy said. "It's more natural to have Kendra playing a game than for us to stand there, staring at the camcorder with nothing to say."

"Keep her under control," Smokey said as he got out his camcorder and fiddled with the settings.

Amy picked up a paper plate. "Remember the boat game?" she asked Kendra.

"Tubby go boat," Kendra said.

"That's right." She held up the paper plate. "This will be the paddle, the same as before. When I say 'paddle,' you make the boat go. Stop when I say 'stop' and paddle over to the door when I say 'door.' Got it?"

Kendra reached for the paper plate.

"Ready?" Amy asked Smokey.

"Go," said Smokey.

Amy handed the plate to Kendra. Speaking toward the camera, she said, "Today we're playing the boat game. Kendra and Tubby are in a pretend boat, and Kendra's going to make it go."

Amy tugged on one earlobe, giving the "sounds like" signal. "Paddle," she said. Kendra began waving the paper plate in big circles, and walking around the table.

Amy said, "Stop!" She looked at the camera as she spoke, and emphasized the word.

Kendra quit walking.

"Good job," Amy said. She tugged her earlobe again. "Paddle," she said.

Kendra began paddling furiously, then broke into a trot. "Stop!" Amy said, but this time Kendra kept going.

Quickly Amy tugged her earlobe, then said, "Door."

Kendra galloped toward the door. "Heehaw!" she shouted.

"Cut!" said Smokey.

"Play something else with her," Hugh said. "She gets crazy playing boat."

"Boat go heehaw!" yelled Kendra.

"That's the end of the boat game," Amy said, reaching for the paper plate.

"Tubby go boat," Kendra said, continuing to run around the cabin.

"I'm going to take her outside for a few minutes," Amy said. "She needs to burn off some energy."

She opened the door. "Let's take Tubby for a walk."

Kendra ran outside, still flailing the paper plate. Amy let her tear around for a few minutes.

Eventually, Kendra slowed down, handed the paper plate to Amy, and said, "Tubby west now."

"I would think so," said Amy. "Let's go back inside, and I'll tell Tubby a story."

They sat by the window, and Amy made up another story about Tubby. This time he went to an ice-cream store and could have any flavor he wanted for his ice-cream cone. Tubby chose Chocolate Chip Cookie Dough.

As before, the two men reviewed the footage together. Amy watched nervously, worried that one of them knew how to play charades and would recognize the "sounds like" signal, but they did not react to her clues. Instead they added the instructions to wait for another DVD.

Smokey put the DVD in a mailing bag, addressed it, and attached postage.

"Go to a different mailbox this time," Hugh said.

"Why don't you go, since you're so fussy?"

Amy tensed, hoping Hugh would refuse.

"I'll stay."

Smokey opened the cabin door.

Hugh went out, too, and headed for the van.

"Where are you going?" Smokey asked.

"To get the gun out of the glove compartment."

It isn't there, Amy thought. I looked in the glove compartment and the gun wasn't there.

"Why?" Smokey asked. "You don't need a gun."

"Neither do you. If you have a problem, you have the car. You can drive off. I have no way to protect myself."

The two men glared at each other for a moment.

"The gun's in the cabin," Smokey said.

"You told me you'd keep it in the van."

"I like to have it inside at night, in case a bear comes around."

"A bear?" Hugh sounded astonished.

"Yeah. I don't like bears."

"There aren't any bears around here," Hugh said.

"Just in case."

"So where's the gun?"

"It's on the floor by the window, under that pile of rags."

Hugh nodded.

Smokey quickly drove away.

Back in the cabin, Hugh went to the pile of rags and lifted them, revealing a black handgun. He shook his head. "Hasn't he ever heard of keeping guns locked away where kids can't find them?"

He put the gun in his jacket pocket.

Amy felt like a balloon with all the air let out. After all her effort, sneaking out in the dark and looking in the van, the gun had been right there within her reach all along. She could easily have taken it and buried it, in less time than she'd spent searching the inside of the van.

The Yellow Cab office reported that the person who had been picked up on Monday at Darielle's address was taken to the airport. There was no record of which airline she had been dropped at.

With hundreds of daily flights, checking passenger lists for her name was a daunting task, and Detective Rockport couldn't be sure she had used her real name. While he waited for the flight lists to be checked, Detective Rockport decided to release Darielle's name to the press.

He called the Edgertons and asked if they might have a photo of Darielle. They did. He drove over to pick it up.

"Have you talked to her?" Mr. Edgerton said.

"Not yet." He told the Edgertons about Amy's clue.

"I can't believe Darielle would be involved in this," Mrs. Edgerton said. "She wasn't a perfect nanny, but she did seem to like Kendra, and I don't see how she could need money."

"Not with what we were paying her," Mr. Edgerton said.

"If Darielle was in on the kidnapping," Mrs. Edgerton said, "she wouldn't have asked for time off on the day that it happened."

Even so, Detective Rockport went back to the station and wrote up a press release, asking anyone with knowledge of Darielle's whereabouts to call. He said Darielle was wanted for questioning as a person of interest in the Edgerton kidnapping case. He also released the photo, which showed Darielle and Kendra sitting by the pool. With any luck, someone would let him know where Darielle was. If she was innocent, she might even call him herself.

Chapter Fifteen

Smokey pulled into the drive-up lane at the post office, and dropped the third DVD into the box. According to the sign on the front of the box, it would be picked up at four-thirty that afternoon.

As he waited to turn back on to the street, he saw a police officer in the rearview mirror. The cop had come out of the post office, but instead of getting in his patrol car, he was looking at the van.

Smokey felt his stomach knot up. By now, the van would be reported as stolen, and the cops probably had the license number. Was this man making the connection?

Smokey made a quick right turn, then a left, then drove a few blocks until he saw a gas station/convenience store. He stopped at one of the gas pumps. Two other vehicles were parked at the pumps. Both were unoccupied; their drivers were inside, paying.

Smokey picked up the newspaper he had bought on the way to the post office, got out, and walked to the closest empty vehicle, a red pickup truck. Peering in, he saw that the keys were in the ignition. He got in, started the truck, and drove off, leaving the white Caravan parked at the gas station.

Smokey drove as fast as he dared, straight out of town. He didn't want to call attention to himself by speeding, but he needed to get away quickly, before the owner of the pickup could give its description and license number to the police.

From now on, Smokey thought, he should probably switch to a new vehicle as soon as he got to town each day. That way he could mail his package without being noticed.

Amy and Kendra were outside, with Hugh watching them, when they heard a vehicle approach.

"Get inside," Hugh said.

The girls went in.

Hugh stood in the doorway, with Amy behind him, peering around his shoulder. When he saw a red pickup, Hugh took out the gun.

"Stay out of sight and don't make any noise," Hugh said. "I'll get rid of whoever this is." He stepped out, closing the door behind him.

Amy went to the window and peeked out. She wondered if she should scream for help. She wished Hugh didn't have the gun.

The pickup rolled to a stop in the same place the van had been parked.

Smokey got out.

Hugh put the gun back in his pocket. "What happened?" he asked. "Where's the van?"

Amy opened the door, wanting to hear Smokey's answer.

"A cop was looking at the van," Smokey said. "It's probably been reported stolen by now, and I thought he might pull me over, so I ditched the van and took this truck."

"A bright red pickup! What's wrong with you? Why didn't you choose a vehicle that wouldn't be so easy to spot?"

"I didn't have a lot of choice." Smokey shrugged. "Besides, I always wanted a red pickup."

Amy's shoulders sagged. She had been so pleased to sneak the white Caravan clue into the DVD, and now it wouldn't do any good.

Hugh rubbed one hand across his mouth, then wiped it on his pant leg. "Did the cop see you?" he asked. "Did he get a look at you?"

"No, he was looking at the van, but it made me nervous."

Amy could tell it made Hugh nervous to hear about it.

"Did you mail it?" Hugh asked.

"That's what I was doing when I saw the cop. I was at the drive-up box, and he was coming out of the post office." He held out the newspaper. "I bought the paper first."

Hugh nodded.

"Tomorrow I'll steal a new car as soon as I get to town, and use it while I mail the next DVD."

"Maybe we shouldn't wait a whole week," Hugh said. "Maybe we should ask for the ransom now."

"Don't go chicken on me," Smokey said.

"Why take more chances than we have to? If you got stopped driving a stolen car, and the cops found an unmailed DVD in your possession, we'd be busted."

"Not going to happen," Smokey said. "I'm too careful."

"Right."

Hugh went inside, sat down, and opened the newspaper. "Still front-page news," he said as he skimmed the article. "No clues. No suspects." He read further. "It doesn't say anything about the first DVD."

"Maybe they didn't get it yet," Smokey said.

"Are you sure you put the right address on it?"

"Of course I'm sure. They probably got it after the paper's deadline."

"I'm going out to the truck," Hugh said. "I want to listen to the news on the radio."

When he returned, Smokey said, "Well? Did you learn anything?"

"The kidnapping is the lead story, but there's no mention of a DVD. I don't like this."

"Sometimes the mail is slow," Smokey said.

"It's not that slow," Hugh said. "They should have two DVDs by now. I thought those films would be played on every TV station in the country, and talked about on all the radio news shows."

"Maybe the kid's parents don't want anyone else to see them."

"That doesn't make sense," Hugh said. "They'd want as many people as possible to know what their daughter looks like."

"As long as the parents see it, that's all I care," Smokey said. "They're the ones with the money. They're the ones who need to get scared."

"They were plenty scared the minute they discovered the kids were gone," Hugh said. "This is fishy. Something isn't right."

Amy didn't say so, but she agreed with Hugh. She had expected the DVDs to be played over and over on TV. She had counted on Jorja figuring out the signals. Now she wondered if Jorja had even seen them.

She watched out the window as fat gray clouds rumbled close, emptied themselves, and drifted away in search of refills. The dark sky matched her mood.

Hugh and Smokey played cards while Amy tried to keep Kendra entertained with Tubby stories.

Late that afternoon the sun returned.

"Being cooped up in here is driving me nuts," Smokey said. "I'm going for a walk." He left, taking the camcorder with him.

Amy took Kendra outside to pick wild clover in the meadow behind the pump.

Hugh sat with his back against the cabin wall, where he could see them.

Amy tied the stem of one clover around another one, knotting it just below the flower. Then she tied another, and another, until she had fashioned a wreath of clover for Kendra to wear on her head.

"You are a princess," Amy said, "with a crown of flowers."

"Tubby like weath," Kendra said.

"Should we make a little wreath for Tubby?"

Kendra grinned, looking as thrilled as if Amy had offered her the queen's jewels.

"You can pick the clover," Amy said. "Get long stems."

While Kendra gathered clover for Tubby, Amy tilted her head back and closed her eyes, letting the sun warm her face. It was pleasant, sitting there in the meadow. She liked the sweet clover smell, and the feel of the tall grass on her arms, and the sound of Kendra murmuring, "Tubby like weath."

Suddenly Amy's eyes flew open. She heard something else, a movement in the woods. Then she heard a voice!

She looked in the direction of the sound.

Hugh must have heard it, too, because he stood up and walked quickly toward Amy.

"Take the kid inside," he said. "Now!"

"Come on, Kendra," Amy said.

"Tubby want weath."

"Bring the clover with you," Amy said. "We'll make Tubby's wreath inside."

As always, Kendra was not easy to hurry. She squatted down in the grass, still searching for long-stemmed clover.

Amy reached down to pick Kendra up. As she did, two women on horseback came into view.

"Stay where you are," Hugh said under his breath. "Don't talk; don't try to signal for help. The gun's in my pocket."

Kendra looked up. "Pony!" she said.

Amy picked up Kendra and turned toward the women. Silently, she pleaded, Look at us! Take a good, close look! We're the girls who were kidnapped, the ones you've heard about on the news, the ones with our pictures in the paper.

The horses stopped as Hugh approached them.

"Hello, ladies," he said. "You lost?"

"No, just out for a ride," one woman replied.

"You're on private property here," Hugh said. "You need to head back that way." He pointed away from the cabin.

"Sorry," the woman said. "We didn't see any 'No Trespassing' sign."

"The wind must have taken my sign down," Hugh said.

The two women turned their horses around and rode away. Although they didn't give any indication that they'd seen Amy standing there with Kendra, Amy thought they must have noticed.

As she put Kendra down, Amy realized her heart was racing.

"Inside," Hugh said.

An hour later, Smokey returned.

"We have to get out of here," Hugh told him. "Tonight."

"What? Why?"

"Two women on horseback rode up while you were gone," Hugh said. He paced around the cabin as he talked. "I got rid of them, but I don't know if they saw the girls or not."

Smokey popped open a can of beer.

Amy held her breath, fearing Smokey would agree to leave. First her arrow was destroyed; then her white Caravan clue wasn't any good. If they left the cabin, her Saddle Stop Store clue would be worthless, too. Even the nanny wouldn't know where to find them if they didn't stay here.

"I don't think the riders saw us," Amy said. "Neither of them even looked my way."

"We can't be sure of that," Hugh said.

"If they had been suspicious," Amy said, "the police would be here by now. Two women out riding in the country would have a cell phone with them. They would have called as soon as they were away from the cabin."

"She's right," Smokey said.

"If one set of horseback riders came past here," Hugh said, "there might be more. We need to get the money, and move on."

"If we leave now, where will we go?" Smokey asked.

"Portland. We'll do everything the way we planned, only a few days sooner. It doesn't make sense to hole up here any longer than we have to."

Smokey sipped his beer. "Okay," he said. "I'm sick of this place, anyhow. We'll make the last DVD and mail it in the morning. We'll say how much money we want, and where to leave it Saturday night. That's two days earlier than we planned."

"We should never have waited this long." Hugh stopped pacing, and looked at Amy. "From now on, you girls stay indoors."

Amy didn't argue. For the first time since they had arrived at the cabin, she felt hope that help would arrive soon. She was certain the women on the horses had seen her and Kendra. They had looked directly at the girls when Kendra said, "Pony."

Surely they would wonder what two girls were doing in this remote cabin. Wouldn't they? Or would they assume that Amy and Kendra were sisters and Hugh was their father? The riders might not have given a second thought to the two girls making clover wreaths beside an old cabin.

Chapter Sixteen

An hour after they left the cabin, Jane and Freida Delane tied their horses to the rail in front of the Saddle Stop Country Store and went inside to buy cold drinks.

"Hey, Leeann," they greeted the clerk.

"Hey. Nice day for a ride." Leeann's lined face was the color of old leather, and her deep, raspy voice gave away her two-pack-a-day habit.

As the sisters paid for their sodas, Jane said, "I see someone's living in the old hunting cabin."

"That so?" said Leeann. "I didn't know that. Who is it?"

"A family. We didn't see the mother, but the father was outdoors with a couple of kids. He told us it was private property and said we should leave," Freida said.

"Not a bit friendly," Jane added.

"Hmm," said Leeann. "Maybe Walt rented the place, although I can't imagine who would pay to live in that dump."

"That's for sure," Jane said. "A couple of my coworkers stayed there once while they were pheasant hunting, and they said it doesn't even have beds."

"Or indoor plumbing," said Leeann.

"Well, to each his own," Freida said. "You'll probably meet the new people, as soon as they run out of something they need."

"Yep," said Leeann, and returned to the magazine she had been reading when the two women entered.

• • •

Mrs. Nordlund spent part of each day at the Edgerton house. So did Jorja and Amy's grandparents. Friends and relatives of both families drifted in and out, bringing food and moral support.

Mrs. Nordlund kept her cell phone on at all times, so if Amy tried to call, it didn't matter whether Mrs. Nordlund was at home or not.

She and Jorja were both at the Edgertons' home on Thursday when Detective Rockport arrived.

"The stolen white Caravan has been found," he said. "It was left in a gas station in Centralia. We believe the man who was driving it stole a red pickup that was parked at the same station."

"Were the girls with him?" Mr. Edgerton asked.

"We don't think so. He switched vehicles so fast, he was probably alone."

"Did anyone see him?" Mrs. Nordlund asked. "Do you have a description?"

"No, but we've dusted the van for fingerprints. Prints from the steering wheel match those from the note the kidnapper left, and from your doorknob."

"Centralia is a long way south of here," Mrs. Edgerton said.

"Yes. The police there are cooperating fully and we've set up a search headquarters there. My partner is on his way down there now with copies of the DVDs."

"If he was alone," Mr. Edgerton said, "where were the girls?"

That night Amy got under the blanket with Kendra, then watched Hugh as he lay down with his own blanket. She had hoped he would take the gun out of his pocket and put it beside him on the floor, but he didn't. He left the gun in his pants pocket, kept his pants on, and crawled under the blanket.

I'll never get it out of his pocket when he's wearing the pants, she thought.

It felt good to lie down, even on the floor. It was tiring to entertain Kendra all day, and be responsible for her. Amy's nervousness wore her out, as well.

At home, Amy usually fell asleep the minute she closed her eyes. In the cabin, lying next to Kendra, her thoughts spun in her mind like Jorja's pet mouse in his exercise wheel.

If her clues had worked, the police knew to question Kendra's nanny and, with luck, they'd figure out that the *paddle-stop-door* sequence meant "Saddle Stop Store."

I've done what I can to help us, Amy thought. Would it be enough?

She tried to think what else she could do. The gun, she decided. She could watch for a chance to steal the gun, and hide it from Hugh and Smokey. She knew her chances of getting killed were a lot higher if Smokey had that gun in his hand than they were without it.

She thought of her dad as she closed her eyes. She recalled Dad telling her, "Never give up, Amy. Even when a situation seems hopeless, take some action to make it better."

At the time, he had been talking about Amy's distress when her best friend in third grade had moved away. The action Amy took back then was to say hi to a girl who was new in her school, and invite the new girl to eat lunch with her. The new girl, Jorja, had said yes, and quickly became Amy's new best friend.

Amy smiled, hearing her dad's voice in her mind. He was big on taking action, she thought. He wouldn't want me to wait around, to see what happens. Wrapped in warm memories, Amy closed her eyes.

The first three nights she had slept only a couple of hours.

Again this night she slept fitfully, waking when she heard Hugh get up, leave the cabin, and return as he did every night.

This time, though, she heard him moving around on the far side of the cabin after he came back. She opened her eyes and turned her head until she could see that he had put a chair in the corner and was standing on it. He held the flashlight in his left hand, pointed at the ceiling. His right hand held the gun.

Amy lay still, hardly daring to breathe. She saw him stretch his right hand up to the top of the old cupboard that hung on the wall. When his hand came down, it was empty.

Amy wasn't sure if he was hiding the gun from Smokey or making certain that she or Kendra couldn't accidentally find it. She closed her eyes and pretended to be asleep.

She heard Hugh move back to his blanket, and lie down.

I know where it is, Amy thought. Now all I need is enough time alone to take it down and get rid of it. That would not be easy. Ever since her attempt to run away, the men had watched her closely.

She estimated it would take her about ten minutes to retrieve the gun, carry it out in the woods, dig a hole, bury it, and return to the cabin.

Amy doubted she would ever have that much time unless she tried to do it in the night. She considered that, but it seemed too risky, with both men sleeping in the cabin, to move the chair and climb on it, and to take the flashlight outside.

One good thing: Smokey probably didn't know where the gun was. He couldn't grab it in a spontaneous fit of rage, and pull the trigger.

Beside her, Kendra whimpered in her sleep. Amy patted Kendra's back, soothing her as she tried to figure out some way to be alone long enough to get rid of the gun.

DAY FIVE

Chapter Seventeen

Mikey Martin always looked for coins. At age five, he had not yet started kindergarten, and he wasn't allowed to cross the street by himself, but he knew that if he checked the area around vending machines, and jiggled the coin returns on pay phones, he often found money, which he used to buy candy at the corner store.

Newspaper and soda machines were his favorite hunting grounds because they required quarters. It was always better to find a quarter than to find a penny or a nickel or a dime. You could get three black licorice sticks for a quarter.

In the week that Mikey had been on vacation with his parents, he had found sixty cents in change, but he didn't know any place in Honolulu where he could go alone to buy candy. He was glad to be going home tonight. Tomorrow he would go to the corner store and spend his fortune.

On his last morning in Hawaii, Mikey wore his black-and-white-striped swimsuit and a blue T-shirt. While his dad paid for their breakfast and his mom waited outside, Mikey set his pail and shovel on the floor, got down on his hands and knees, and fished two quarters out from under the newspaper machine. He couldn't add high enough to know what that brought his total to, but he knew it was a lot, the most he'd ever had at one time.

Grinning, he stood and opened his backpack. He put the two quarters in the zippered pouch where he kept his found money.

As he slipped the backpack on again, he glanced at the front page of the newspaper. A photo showed a woman and a little girl, sitting by a pool. The woman looked familiar, but Mikey couldn't think where he had seen her. He didn't know the little girl.

"Come on, Mikey," his dad said. "Mom's waiting."

They walked out the back door of the hotel, directly onto the white, sandy beach. Mikey loved the beach. He liked filling his bucket with sand, then dumping it out. He liked wading in the warm water, or sitting at the edge, letting the waves wash up across his legs. The only part Mikey didn't like was getting slathered with sunscreen, but his mom didn't give him a choice about that.

While Mikey played in the sand, his parents sat nearby on identical purple towels, reading magazines.

Two hours later, Mikey saw the woman. He had finally grown tired of shoveling sand and was heading toward his mom and dad to see if they would buy him an ice-cream cone, when he saw the blond lady, sitting in one of the low canvas beach chairs, sunning herself. Mikey stopped and looked at her more closely. Then he ran to his parents.

"That lady's picture is in the paper," Mikey said, pointing at the blond woman.

"Shh," his mother said. "It isn't polite to point."

Mikey put his hand down. "Her picture's in the paper," he repeated. "I saw it."

Mikey's parents looked at the woman.

"I don't recognize her," Mr. Martin said. "Do you?"

"No," Mrs. Martin said, "but she's pretty enough to be an actress. Lots of movie and TV stars vacation here."

"When did you see her picture?" Mr. Martin asked.

"This morning, when I was looking for money by the newspaper machine."

"Wouldn't that be something," Mrs. Martin said, "if we saw someone famous? Maybe we should go over there and ask for her autograph. We could sell it on eBay."

"We can't ask for an autograph if we don't know who she is."

"She looks like a celebrity," Mrs. Martin said.

They watched the blond woman for a few minutes, but since neither of them could come up with a name, they decided against approaching her.

Mrs. Martin checked the time, and gasped. "It's eleven-thirty!" she said.

The Martins left the beach in a rush, took quick showers in their room, and checked out. The shuttle to the airport arrived at twelve-fifteen.

While they waited for their flight, Mrs. Martin bought a newspaper. When she started to read it, she saw the picture that Mikey had seen earlier.

"Look at this," she said, handing the paper to her husband. "I think it's the woman we saw at the beach."

They both read the article that accompanied the photo.

"She didn't have a child with her," Mr. Martin said. "Mikey, did you see a little girl with that woman?"

"No," Mikey said.

"It doesn't say she's accused of being the kidnapper," Mrs. Martin said. "She's the girl's nanny. She's a person of interest, wanted for questioning."

They studied the picture again.

"Maybe we should call the police," Mrs. Martin said.

"We left the beach two hours ago," Mr. Martin said. "She might not still be there."

"She comes every day," Mikey said.

"They could watch for her," Mrs. Martin said. "It would be a stakeout, like in the movies."

The gate attendant announced that Flight 243 was boarding at Gate Seven.

"That's us," Mr. Martin said.

Mrs. Martin laid the newspaper on the empty chair beside her, picked up her carry-on bag, and said, "Come on, Mikey. It's time to get on the airplane."

Holding his mother's hand, Mikey walked down the tunnel and boarded the plane.

It wasn't until they were buckled into their seats that Mrs. Martin said, "I left the newspaper in the terminal."

"If it's the same woman," Mr. Martin said, "someone else will recognize her. I don't want to get involved in a police investigation. They might ask us to delay our flight home."

"It probably wasn't even her," Mrs. Martin said.

Chapter Eighteen

On Friday, the temperature climbed to eighty-three degrees, making the small cabin feel stifling. No matter what activity Amy suggested, Kendra didn't want to do it. Amy tried to be patient.

"Tubby want ice cweam," Kendra said.

"As soon as you get home, you can have ice cream."

"Tubby go home now."

Amy wished she had a way to make Kendra understand. "I want to go home, too," she said. "We'll go as soon as we can."

"Tubby do potty in pants," Kendra said.

Amy looked in dismay at the large wet spot on Kendra's overalls. She took Kendra out to the well, stripped her clothes off, and said, "We're going to take a shower."

"Tubby want bathtub."

"I don't have a bathtub," Amy said, "but the water will feel good on this hot day." She started pumping, and let Kendra splash in the water. Kendra was tentative at first, sticking one hand in the water, and then one foot. Eventually, she put her head under the spigot, squealing as the water cascaded over her.

"Now I'm going to wash your clothes," Amy said. She scrubbed Kendra's underpants and draped them on some tall weeds in the sun to dry. She washed the little girl's overalls, too, and the formerly white T-shirt that was now gray and covered with food smears. Without soap, the clothes didn't look much better, but at least they didn't smell anymore.

Kendra jumped in the puddles, holding Tubby over her head so he didn't get wet.

Amy wanted to rinse out her own clothes, too, but she had nothing else to wear and she wasn't going to wait around naked while her clothes dried. Not with Hugh and Smokey watching every move she made.

While she waited for Kendra's clothes to dry, she got the pan Smokey had bought, filled it with water, and let Kendra dribble water on the clover. "Give the flowers a drink," Amy said, and Kendra happily played this new game, filling the pan over and over.

Kendra's clothes dried quickly in the heat, but when Amy tried to put them back on her, Kendra said, "Tubby want sunsuit. Put on pink sunsuit."

Amy sighed. She wished she could produce Kendra's pink sunsuit, which was no doubt folded neatly in a dresser drawer in Kendra's bedroom.

"Soon you'll be home," she said. "Then you can wear anything you want. For now, this is all you have."

Kendra's bottom lip quivered. "Tubby want Mommy," she said.

"Me, too," Amy said, fighting back her own tears. She wished she could take a shower and put on clean clothes. My khaki shorts, Amy thought, and my green tank top would be perfect today.

It was nearly time for Kendra's nap. Amy decided to give her a snack, and then see if she would fall asleep outside, where a slight breeze made it a little cooler than in the cabin.

As she approached the front of the cabin, she heard the truck's engine start. Was Smokey leaving again? Amy looked at the vehicle and saw that Hugh and Smokey were sitting in the pickup, with the engine running. She waited, but they didn't drive away.

She realized they were running the air-conditioning, trying to get cool. She and Kendra had stayed around the pump area for so long that the men had quit watching them.

This is my chance, Amy thought.

Amy took Kendra inside, and quickly gave her a box of crackers.

Amy breathed faster. She looked out the window. Both men were still in the truck.

While Kendra helped herself to some crackers, Amy carried the wooden chair to the corner where she'd seen Hugh stand on it in the night. She climbed on the chair, and reached her hand up to the top of the cupboard. Instantly, her fingers closed around the gun.

She got down, and pushed the chair back to the table, keeping her back to Kendra so the little girl didn't see what she held.

Amy stared at the black metal weapon in her hand. A feeling of power surged through her. If she chose to, she could walk outside right now, point the gun at Hugh and Smokey, and demand that they drive her and Kendra home.

Better still, she'd have them drive only to the Saddle Stop Country Store, where Amy and Kendra would get out, and Amy could go inside and call the police.

But what if they called her bluff? Hugh might do what she said, once the gun was pointed at him, but Smokey was likely to lunge at her and try to take the gun away. What then?

She did not want to kill anybody, not even Smokey. He was a slime bag, and Hugh was no saint, either, but they were still human beings. No matter how mean they were, Amy did not want to end their lives.

There was always the possibility, too, that Smokey would succeed in getting the gun away from her. He was far bigger and stronger than she was. If he wrestled it out of her grasp, she knew he'd have no qualms about pulling the trigger. Or it could go off accidentally while they struggled. What if, without intending to, they shot Kendra?

Amy's hands shook.

Instead of using the gun, she wanted to get rid of it, to hide it some place where the men would never find it. That way it wouldn't kill or injure anyone.

She knew she didn't have much time. They had not noticed her and Kendra come inside, but they would soon, and would come to check on what she was doing.

Her original plan, if she had found the gun the night she looked for it in the car, had been to bury it far out in the woods. She didn't have time for that now. If she buried the gun, it would have to be near the cabin, and they'd see the freshly dug dirt, and would dig it up.

She heard the car doors slam.

The men were coming.

There was no place to hide the gun inside the cabin.

"Tubby go potty," Kendra said.

That will buy me some time to think, Amy decided. She concealed the gun inside her shirt, opened the door just as Hugh and Smokey got there, and said, "I'm taking Kendra to the bathroom."

"Okay," Hugh said.

The two girls walked the short distance to the outhouse, and Amy helped Kendra with her clothes.

"Potty stink," Kendra said.

And that's when Amy knew she'd found the perfect place to get rid of the gun. Yes! she thought. They'll never look down there.

"Go outside and wait for me, where it doesn't smell," she told Kendra. She knew it would be best if Kendra didn't know anything about the gun. When the men realized the gun was gone, and started asking questions, and looking for it, Amy didn't want Kendra to give away the fact that Amy had taken the gun.

Kendra went out.

Amy closed the outhouse door.

She took the handgun out from under her shirt, held it over the vile-smelling hole for an instant, and let go. She heard the dull *thunk* when it landed.

Even if Smokey or Hugh thought to look for it there, she was sure they'd never attempt to get it back. She opened the door, smiling, and stepped back into the sunlight.

Amy whistled on her way back to the cabin, and didn't mind the heat at all.

She carried her blanket outside and spread it in the shade, making a place for Kendra to take her nap. Kendra, clutching Tubby, curled on her side while Amy sat beside her, singing softly.

Tubby is a good cat, good cat, good cat,
Tubby is a good cat, good little cat.

It was a song Amy's dad used to sing to her when she was little. He had used the name of her favorite doll instead of Tubby, and she had loved the simple song. Kendra liked it, too.

Kendra was soon asleep.

While Kendra slept, Amy watched Hugh and Smokey make the last DVD. Smokey kept the camcorder pointed at the sleeping Kendra, so there was no action to watch, but Amy knew that anyone looking at this video would have their attention riveted on what was being said.

"We want five hundred thousand dollars in cash," Smokey said. "Unmarked bills. Fifties and hundreds, no bigger bills. Bring the money at midnight on Saturday to the public library in Chehalis. Come alone, put the container of money by the front door, leave immediately. Do not tell the police."

Smokey paused for a moment, then said, "I repeat: Do not tell the police. There are two of us, but only one will come to pick up the money. The other will stay with Kendra. If the one with Kendra does not get a call by twelve-ten, saying that his partner has the cash and is on his way with it, you won't see your daughter again."

Smokey continued: "If you obey our instructions and we are not followed, Kendra will be released at a safe place within an hour. We aren't saying where because we don't want that place watched, but she will be unhurt and the people who find her will notify you right away."

Amy noticed that Smokey said nothing about her. The instructions were for Kendra's parents and he said they'd be releasing Kendra. She knew Smokey didn't talk about where she would be released, because letting her go was not part of the plan.

She watched Smokey put this DVD in a mailing envelope, knowing it was the final film.

"Be careful," Hugh said. "Watch your mirrors. And get a different car. We can't leave here in the pickup."

"I'll switch cars as soon as I get to town," Smokey said.

"How can you steal a car so easily?" Amy asked.

"People are stupid. They go inside a store and leave the engine running. In cold weather, they start the car in their driveway and go inside while the car warms up. Anybody can jump in the car and drive off."

"Just be sure there's no baby in the backseat," Hugh said. "We have enough kids to deal with."

Smokey left.

"That happened once," Hugh said. "He stole a car and got four blocks down the street before he realized there was a baby in a car seat."

"What happened?"

"He ditched the car and the baby in a parking lot, and stole a different car. Probably the only smart move he ever made."

This seems like a normal conversation, Amy thought. Whenever Smokey was away, she and Hugh talked almost as if they were friends. Yet she knew he expected her to be dead before he left the cabin. He wouldn't do it himself, but he wouldn't prevent Smokey from doing it.

Amy wondered what would happen if she offered Hugh a bargain. If he let her live, she would promise to tell the police that there was only one kidnapper: Smokey. She thought Kendra was too young to be questioned. Amy was the only witness.

If the police weren't looking for Hugh, he could take his share of the money and start his life over. He had said he wanted to stay out of trouble, that all he needed was a chance. Maybe Amy should offer him that chance, in return for her own life.

In order for such an agreement to work, Hugh would have to trust her to keep her promise. Would he?

What if Smokey got caught and then he implicated Hugh? If that happened, the police would find out that Amy had lied. What if Amy was asked to take a lie detector test?

Should she lie for Hugh, in order to save herself?

All her life, Amy had been taught to be truthful. If her dad was still living, what would he say if he knew she had intentionally let a kidnapper go free? Would he be relieved to have her home, regardless of what it took to get her there, or would this be another occasion for him to be ashamed of her?

If Hugh sincerely wanted to start over and not get in trouble,

Amy decided, he would not have agreed to help Smokey with the kidnapping. Smokey used his unhappy childhood as an excuse to commit crimes, and Hugh used the difficulty of being an ex-con as his excuse.

Just like I used having unexpected company as an excuse to forget about Lucky that night, Amy thought.

From now on, she decided, there would be no excuses, and no lies. There would be no deal with Hugh—which meant she still needed to figure out a way to save herself.

Today was Friday. She had until midnight Saturday to be found. Tomorrow.

If the women on horseback had called the police to report that they had seen two girls the ages of the kidnapped girls, with a man in a remote cabin, help would have arrived by now.

I'm running out of options, Amy thought. Nothing I've tried has worked, and I don't know what else to do, and my time is almost up.

Chapter Nineteen

Jane Delane glanced at the photo in the newspaper. Then she put on her reading glasses and scrutinized the picture carefully.

"Look at this, Freida," she said.

Her sister looked up from her knitting.

Jane passed her the newspaper. "Look at that photo. Is that the little girl we saw by the old cabin?"

Freida looked at the picture. "Hard to say," she said.

"I think it might be," Jane said. "The missing girls are fourteen and three. Those kids looked about that age. The older one was holding the little one. Remember?"

"I didn't notice," Freida said. "I was looking at their dad."

"I wonder if we should call the police," Jane said.

"Oh, for goodness' sake," Freida said. "Don't get all melodramatic. Just because we happened to see two children doesn't mean it was the girls who were kidnapped. What would they be doing in that dilapidated old place?"

"Hiding? Maybe that wasn't their father. Maybe it was the kidnapper."

"Remember the last time you called the police, when you were certain the clerk in the 7-Eleven was the man you'd seen on *America's Most Wanted*?"

"Anyone can make a mistake."

"Make enough of them and the police won't come if we ever really need them. They'll think it's your imagination again."

“I suppose you’re right,” Jane said. “Would you like some tea?”

Detective Rockport watched the third DVD with the Edgertons, Amy’s mother, and Jorja. The signal wasn’t quite the same this time. Instead of scratching first one ear and then the other, Amy tugged on one earlobe. If that was the signal, her message eluded them.

She did it before she said “paddle,” and she did it again before she said “door.” Paddle door? It meant nothing.

She also emphasized the word *stop,* but no one found any hidden meaning there, either. They all agreed: these new clues, if that’s what they were, didn’t make any sense.

“Maybe there isn’t any clue this time,” Detective Rockport said.

“If there’s no clue,” Mrs. Nordlund said, “you can release this video to the media. Maybe someone will recognize where it was made.”

“Having something new to report will put the story at the top of the news again,” Mrs. Edgerton said. “We want people to keep watching for Kendra and Amy.”

They played the video again.

Suddenly Jorja said, “I think she’s giving the ‘sounds like’ signal, from charades!”

“The what signal?” asked Detective Rockport.

“It’s used in the game, charades,” Jorja said, “where you act out a book, song, or movie title and the others try to guess what it is.”

“I played that in college,” Mr. Edgerton said. “If you tug on your earlobe, it means the word you act out next sounds like the word you want your team to guess.”

“That’s right,” Jorja said. “If you want them to say ‘fat,’ you could pull on your ear and then get down on your hands and knees and rub against someone's ankles, and they would say, 'cat,' and you'd nod yes. Then they'd know the word you want sounds like *cat*."

"So she's telling us the words she wants sound like *paddle* and *door*," Detective Rockport said.

"Exactly," said Jorja.

"Okay," said Mrs. Edgerton. "Everybody write down all the words you can think of that rhyme with *paddle* and *door*. Then we'll try to make some sense of the possibilities."

"She emphasizes *stop*," Mrs. Nordlund said. "In between *paddle* and *door*, she stresses the word *stop*."

"But she doesn't give the 'sounds like' signal then," Mr. Edgerton said.

"No, she doesn't."

Detective Rockport decided not to release this DVD yet. If Amy had sent more clues, he didn't want to tip off the kidnapper. He left to show the DVD to the other members of his squad, leaving the girls' families writing out lists of words.

Jeff finished his meeting early and decided to surprise Darielle by joining her at the beach. As he walked through the hotel lobby he took one of the complimentary newspapers. He wanted to check the financial markets while he sat in the sun.

He set his folding beach chair beside Darielle's and began to read. A few minutes later, he gasped. "Darielle! Your picture is in the newspaper!"

"Mine?" She sat up. "What for?"

"It says the police want to question you. They believe you might have information about that kidnapping."

Darielle's mind went into overdrive. She had assumed that

without her, Smokey would abandon his plan to steal Kendra, but he must have gone ahead.

"What kidnapping?" she asked.

"The Edgerton girl. Haven't you heard it on the news? It's been the lead story ever since we got here."

"I'm on vacation. I haven't listened to any news."

"The daughter of Kurt and Elyse Edgerton was kidnapped, along with her babysitter. The police want to ask you about it."

"Kendra's been kidnapped?" She said it as if she were horrified, as if such a possibility had never occurred to her before. If Jeff found out that she had a part in this, her dreams of a future as a pampered wife would be over. "Why would the police want to talk to me?"

He frowned at her. "It says you're the child's nanny."

She had not told Jeff about her job. Instead, she had hinted that she was independently wealthy, thanks to a family business started by her great-grandfather. "I stayed with Kendra a few times, as a favor to her mother," Darielle said.

He removed a cell phone from his pocket. "Here," he said. "You had better call right away."

Darielle had no intention of talking to the police. She certainly wasn't going to tell them about Smokey. The plan had been to keep Kendra for a week and then, when the ransom was paid, to let her go. Smokey had promised that the child would not be hurt.

If she said nothing, she could still collect the money Smokey had promised her. Even though she had not been there the day he took Kendra, she had given him the layout of the Edgertons' house, which showed exactly where Kendra's room was, and she had told him what time the little girl took her nap. She had even let him copy the house key. Without her help, Smokey could not have pulled it off, so she deserved her share even though she had not been there. Darielle had nothing to gain by letting the police know who the kidnapper was.

She realized she had the perfect alibi. She and Jeff had been on the plane en route to Hawaii when Kendra was stolen.

She wondered if Smokey was hiding Kendra in the old hunting cabin that belonged to Darielle's uncle, as they had intended. If so, it was all the more reason why she should get her payoff after he collected the ransom.

Darielle took the cell phone, and stood up so Jeff couldn't see her hands. She pretended to dial, then identified herself and explained that she'd seen the newspaper request for information about her.

She covered the phone with her hand and told Jeff, "They're transferring me."

For the next few minutes, Darielle faked a conversation. She explained where she was and why. She said she had not known about the kidnapping until just before she called, and swore she had no idea who might have done it. There had been no odd phone calls to the Edgerton house while she was there, nor had she ever noticed anyone lurking around.

She gave Jeff's cell-phone number and said she'd be glad to answer any further questions. She said she'd be back at her own apartment on Sunday, and promised to call again then. Finally she pretended to end the call, and handed the phone back to Jeff.

"Poor Kendra," she said. "That darling little girl! And her mother! Elyse must be frantic." She pretended to choke back a sob, and Jeff wrapped his arms around her.

"There, there," he said. "The police are working on it. They'll probably find her soon."

"That precious child!"

"I didn't realize you knew the Edgertons," Jeff said.

"Elyse and I have been friends since college," Darielle said.

"I never met her," Jeff said, "but Kurt and I invested in an apartment building together several years ago. We kept it for a while, then sold it for a nice profit. He's a good man."

"I can't bear to talk about it," Darielle said as she wiped her eyes.

"We won't mention it again," Jeff promised.

Darielle looked somber, but inside she was cheering. Not only had she gained Jeff's sympathy, she would be getting $50,000 from Smokey. A rich boyfriend, and money of her own, too. What more could she want?

One of the other police detectives figured out the right combination of "sounds like" words.

"There's an old place down in Lewis County called Saddle Stop Country Store," he told Detective Rockport. "My brother-in-law looked at some property down there a few months ago, and I went with him. We took a wrong turn and ended up stopping at this ramshackle store to ask directions. I'm almost certain it was called the Saddle Stop Country Store."

"Amy didn't say anything that sounds like *country*," Detective Rockport said.

"No, she didn't. But I can't think of any words that rhyme with *country*; maybe she couldn't, either. Maybe *Saddle Stop Store* was as close as she could get."

"I'll check it out. Where exactly is this place?"

The detective called his brother-in-law, and then gave directions that were as close as the two men could remember.

Detective Rockport got there about three hours later. As he parked his car, he felt as if he'd stepped back in time fifty years. He went inside, and showed his identification to the woman behind the counter.

"Mind if I ask you a few questions?" he said.

"I have all day. Ask away."

"Your name?"

"Leeann Dinwiddy."

"You own this place?"

"Yep. My granddaddy built it and then my mama ran it, and now it's mine."

"Has anyone come in recently with two young girls?"

"Nope."

"Any customers in the last few days that you didn't know?"

"A few. But I get a lot of customers I don't know. There are some RVs parked at the lake a few miles east of here that get rented out to folks who fish. They come in for supplies. There are only a handful of regulars, who live around here."

Detective Rockport saw a display of balls, action figures, and other inexpensive toys—the sort of thing parents buy on impulse when their kids beg. "Have you sold any of the toys this week?"

"Nope."

"Has anyone asked to buy something out of the ordinary?"

Leeann thought for a moment. "One guy wanted padded envelopes. The kind you mail stuff in."

Detective Rockport gripped his pen. "When was this?"

"A couple of days ago. Can't say for sure."

"What did he look like?"

"Young man, in his twenties. None too clean. Fidgety. He wouldn't look me in the eye."

"How tall?"

"About six foot. Don't ask me what he weighed. I didn't look that close."

"What color hair?

"Dark. Kind of long and stringy."

"Did you happen to notice what he was driving?"

Leeann shook her head. "I don't pay much attention to cars," she said. "Use a horse, myself."

"Did he have any distinguishing marks? A scar? Tattoo?"

"No, nothing like that. He came in twice. The first time he bought some food, and the next time he asked about the envelopes. I haven't seen him since."

Detective Rockport wrote his cell-phone number on the back of his business card. "If you see him again," he said, "please call me. Anytime, day or night. Don't let him hear you."

"Is he wanted for something?" she asked.

"Maybe. I'd like to talk to him."

Leeann tucked the card into her shirt pocket.

"Thanks for your help," Detective Rockport said. "Please call if you remember anything else unusual that has happened."

As soon as he got in his car, he ordered a helicopter search of the woods around the Saddle Stop Country Store.

Leeann watched the squad car drive away. Later that day she replayed the conversation in her mind. The cop had asked if two girls had come in. She wondered if she should have told him about the children Freida and Jane had seen by the old cabin. Of course that was yesterday. They could be long gone by now.

She took the card from her pocket and looked at it, wondering if she should call. He had asked her to let him know if that man who wanted envelopes came back. He hadn't asked her to call if she saw some kids, and she hadn't actually seen them herself. Leeann had never been one to pass along gossip, unless she knew for certain that it was true. She put the card back in her pocket.

Chapter Twenty

Kendra and Amy were sitting on the blanket outlining a "house" for Tubby out of rocks when the first helicopter flew over.

Hugh, who had stretched out on the ground not far away, leaped to his feet as soon as he heard the chopper approaching.

"Get inside," he barked. "Now!"

He picked up Kendra and ran for the cabin. "Bring the blanket!" he called.

Looking skyward, Amy gathered the blanket, dumping the rock house. She heard the helicopter but couldn't yet see it. She longed to stay outside, and wave the blanket in a big circle over her head, to attract attention.

But Hugh had Kendra. Reluctantly, she followed him inside.

They listened as the helicopter roared over, flying low.

"It's a good thing Smokey isn't here," Hugh muttered. "No car." A moment later he added, "No smoke coming out of the chimney. The place will look unoccupied."

The helicopter had flown toward the cabin from the direction of the main road. It passed over once, then circled around and flew over a second time. After that, it continued going east.

As soon as it was gone, Hugh dragged a chair over to the cupboard, climbed on it, and reached up to the top. Amy busied herself folding the blanket and pretended not to notice as Hugh felt along the top of the cupboard.

He got off the chair, and glared at Amy, his hands on his hips. "Where is it?" he demanded.

Amy hoped she looked innocent. "Where is what?"

"The gun. What have you done with the gun?"

"I don't know what you're talking about. I don't have the gun. I thought Smokey kept it in the car."

"It's gone," Hugh said. "I hid it on top of the cupboard, and now it's gone."

"Smokey must have taken it," Amy said.

"He didn't know where it was."

"Neither did I."

"When would he have taken it? I've been with him the whole time." Hugh's eyes narrowed as he leaned closer to Amy. "You snooped around in here while we were cooling off in the car, and you found the gun."

"I wish you were right," Amy said, "but if I had found the gun, I would have used it to get myself out of here."

He looked uncertain. "Yes," he said, "I suppose you would have."

"It wouldn't do me any good to take it and not use it," Amy said.

Hugh's anger flashed again. "That sneak!" he said. "I wonder when he found it."

"He probably found it while we were outside," Amy said. "He stays in here by himself a lot, playing solitaire."

"He took the gun with him," Hugh said, "and left me here with no way to defend myself."

Hugh began walking back and forth. "Where is he? It doesn't take this long to mail a package. He's so trigger-happy, he probably fired the gun and got himself caught. He'll blow the whole plan!"

Amy knew Smokey wouldn't shoot the gun because he didn't have it, but she couldn't say that so she let Hugh fret.

Hugh paced around the cabin like a caged lion. Each time he passed the window, he peered anxiously outside. "He should have been back by now," he said. "Where is he?"

Amy knew he didn't expect an answer.

When Smokey finally arrived, in a black sedan, Hugh rushed out to greet him.

"Park back in the trees," he said, "where the car won't be so easy to spot from the air."

"Why? What's going on?"

"They're looking for us," Hugh said. "A helicopter went over, flying real low. I'm certain he spotted the cabin."

"It was probably the Forest Service, checking for fires," Smokey said.

"We're leaving," Hugh said. "We're out of here."

"Now? I just mailed the ransom DVD. We don't get the money till tomorrow at midnight. Where are we going to go?"

"I don't know. We'll sleep in the car. Anything! But we have to get out of here. Those women on the horses must have called the cops."

"You're paranoid," Smokey said.

Hugh went around to the passenger side of the car, opened it, and then unlatched the glove compartment. "Where is it?" he asked.

"Where is what?" Smokey said.

"Don't give me that," Hugh said. "I know you found the gun. What have you done with it?" A look of horror crossed his face. "You didn't leave it in the pickup, did you? Because if you did . . ."

"I put the gun under the pile of rags. Remember? I said I

wanted it inside, in case a bear came in the night, and you said okay but you had to be in charge of it."

"And I hid it on top of the cupboard, and when I went to get it back, it wasn't there, so don't act innocent. We don't have time to play games."

Smokey looked from Hugh to Amy. "Hey, man," he said. "If you hid the gun and now it isn't there, you'd better talk to our friend here, because I never took it."

"He's lying," Amy said. "Believe me, if I had found the gun, I wouldn't still be sitting around in this cabin."

"You probably forgot where you hid it," Smokey said.

"I didn't forget!" Hugh said.

"Let's eat," Smokey said, "and then we can look for the gun. I went to the drive-through and got burgers."

"Haven't you been listening?" Hugh said. "We are leaving! Now! So get whatever you want from the cabin and bring it out to the car."

"You're serious," Smokey said.

"Move it."

Amy inched toward the car until she was close enough to look in. As she had hoped, the keys hung from the ignition.

She watched Hugh go back in the cabin. Smokey headed that way, too, rooting around in the white bag that he held. Kendra was between Smokey and Amy, pretending that Tubby was dancing in the grass.

Now's my chance, Amy thought. If I can get in the car without Smokey noticing, I can drive away.

First, she had to get Kendra in the car.

She didn't want to talk because she didn't want to call Smokey's attention back to her. She waved her arms at Kendra, and then, when the child looked at her, she motioned for Kendra to come.

Kendra ambled that way, still making Tubby dance.

Amy held her breath, willing Kendra to hurry. She wanted to yell, "Run! Get in the car!" but she clamped her lips together and waited.

Smokey fished a container of french fries out of the bag and ate one. He was near the door of the cabin.

When Kendra was almost to the car, Amy quietly opened the front door, and slid behind the steering wheel. She motioned for Kendra to climb into the car with her.

Kendra said, "Tubby go bye-bye?"

As soon as Kendra spoke, Smokey looked back. Immediately, he dropped the white bag and rushed toward Kendra.

"Get in!" Amy said, reaching out to grasp the toddler's hands and pull her in. "Hurry!"

As Kendra reached up to take Amy's hand, she dropped Tubby. Instead of letting Amy pull her into the car without him, Kendra let go of Amy's hands and stooped to pick him up.

That gave Smokey just enough time. He pulled a knife from his pocket, switched the blade open, and pointed the tip at Kendra.

"Where is my gun?" he asked Amy.

"I don't have it," Amy said.

"You took it. You know where it is."

"I don't know! Hugh must have forgotten where he put it."

Kendra stood up, holding Tubby.

Smokey kept the tip of the knife inches from her neck. "Get out of the car," he told Amy. His voice shook with anger. She saw the fury in his cold, dark eyes. She knew if she did what he said, her life was over. If she didn't obey him, he would hurt Kendra.

Instead of getting out, Amy jerked her head and gasped, looking off to the side as if she saw something in the woods. Then she screamed—a piercing, bloodcurdling shriek, and pointed over Smokey's shoulder, into the trees.

"A bear!" she shouted. "Run! There's a huge black bear coming!"

Chapter Twenty-one

Smokey never looked. The second he heard *bear*, he bolted toward the cabin as fast as he could run.

Amy grabbed Kendra, pulled her into the car, and locked the doors. At the same time, Smokey closed the door of the cabin behind him.

Amy turned the key, and the engine started. The shift arrow was on *P*. Amy didn't know what that meant, but one of the other choices was *D*, and she hoped that meant "Drive." She pushed the stick until the arrow pointed to *D*, then put her foot on the gas pedal, and pressed.

The car leaped forward. Kendra lost her balance and braced her hands on the dashboard.

"Try to put your seat belt on," Amy said.

Amy turned the wheel. When the front end of the car was aimed approximately at the lane, she straightened out the wheel and hoped for the best.

She heard shouts from the cabin. Looking over her shoulder, she saw Hugh explode out the door, and run toward the car. Amy pushed her foot harder on the gas pedal and the car shot down the road.

"Tubby go home?" Kendra said.

"I hope so," Amy said.

She had to be sure she knew how to stop, so she didn't hit anything. She tentatively tapped the other pedal and the car jerked as it slowed. Okay, that was the brake.

She pushed on the gas some more. She didn't dare look back to see how close Hugh was; she needed to concentrate on steering.

If she could just make it out to the main road, she'd flag down the first vehicle she saw. If there weren't any, she'd go all the way to the Saddle Stop Country Store.

They jerked and jostled. Amy gripped the steering wheel so hard that her fingers ached.

"Tubby go fast!" said Kendra as she bounced up and down on the seat, clearly enjoying the wild ride.

After what seemed an eternity, Amy saw the road ahead. She slowed, looked both ways, and carefully turned. The car went too far and crossed over the center line. Amy made a quick correction. Driving wasn't as simple as it looked.

It was easier to steer on the paved road than it had been on the gravel, but she had gone only a few yards when the engine sputtered, then died. The car rolled to a stop.

Amy turned the key. It made a grinding sound. Had she done something wrong? Had she wrecked the engine?

She looked at the dials on the dashboard, and noticed that one was a half-moon dial with *F* on the right end and *E* on the left. An arrow was past the *E*. The gas tank, Amy thought. *F* means "Full" and *E* means "Empty," and Smokey had not had the sense to buy gas.

She debated whether she and Kendra should walk, or sit in the car and wait to be found. She preferred to wait, but what if Hugh and Smokey got there before anyone else? Even a locked door wouldn't keep them out.

While she hesitated, she heard the helicopter again. Amy got out of the car. "Sit where I was," she told Kendra. "Honk the horn."

Kendra scrambled into the driver's seat.

"Go ahead," Amy said. "Honk it as much as you want."

"Tubby like noise," Kendra said, and she began pounding the horn, over and over.

Amy waved her arms over her head. She ran back and forth beside the car, hoping that the movement would attract attention. The helicopter approached, circled, and went over again.

Amy waved, and shouted until she was hoarse, although she knew the pilot couldn't hear her over the noise of the engine.

Kendra continued to honk the horn.

The chopper flew away. Had the pilot seen her? Was he looking for a place to land? Had he radioed for someone to come and help her?

Ahead, at the Saddle Stop Country Store, Leeann walked out onto the porch and watched the helicopter go over. They're looking for someone, she thought. That's the second helicopter in the last hour. Whoever they were looking for must be important.

She remembered the two children that Freida and Jane had seen. She thought about the girls who had been kidnapped; she'd read about them last night in the newspaper. It might be better, she decided, to pass along a rumor than not to give out information that might prove to be crucial.

She went back inside and dialed the number on the back of the officer's card. When he answered, she said, "This is Leeann, at the Saddle Stop Country Store. There's an old cabin near here, and someone told me they saw two girls there."

Detective Rockport felt the gooseflesh rise on his arms. He was already in the area, at the helicopter launch site.

"It's an old hunting cabin," Leeann explained. "It's owned by Walter Monroe, but he never uses it anymore. A couple of the locals were out there riding horses and said they saw a man with two young girls."

"Where is it? How do I get there?"

She told him.

Detective Rockport called for backup, and took off. A minute later he got a call on his radio from one of the helicopter pilots.

"There's a car parked on the road, about three miles from the Saddle Stop," he said. "It's in the middle of the road and someone's waving and trying get my attention. It looks like a kid."

Amy was sure the helicopter pilot had seen her. The copter had circled around more than once before it flew away. She got back in the car and locked the doors, hoping help would arrive before Hugh did.

Amy heard the siren before she saw the black-and-white police car headed toward her, its lights whirling. She waited until the officer stopped the car and got out before she unlocked her door.

Detective Rockport said, "Amy Nordlund?"

Amy nodded, unable to speak over the lump in her throat.

"I am very glad to see you," he said. "I'm Detective Rockport." She saw him look past her, into the car.

"Kendra's with me," Amy said. "She's fine. We're both okay."

"Where is the kidnapper?"

"There are two of them."

Two other squad cars arrived, responding to Detective Rockport's call for backup. Amy told them where Hugh and Smokey were, and the officers took off down the gravel road.

Detective Rockport said, "Get in my car. You can call your mom, and I'll talk to Kendra's parents before I drive you home."

"We're going to ride in the police car," Amy told Kendra.

Kendra grinned at Detective Rockport. "Tubby do honk?" she asked.

Gasping for breath, Hugh ran after the black sedan. He stopped when he heard the police cars coming. For a moment he considered trying to hide in the woods, but he knew it was useless. If he hid, they'd bring in search dogs.

Even if he somehow got away, he had no money, no means of transportation, nowhere to go except back to prison.

I should never have agreed to help Smokey, Hugh thought. Even if Darielle had stayed around, the plan would not have worked. The cops aren't stupid; they would have figured out that Darielle was the one delivering the videos and they would have followed her. I let wishful thinking push out my common sense.

He stood in the middle of the road with his hands over his head, and watched the police come forward to arrest him.

Smokey stayed in the cabin, looking nervously out the window for a bear. Even after he realized Amy had probably tricked him, he was uneasy about going out. He wished he knew where the gun was. If he had a gun, he wouldn't be afraid of a bear.

As the police cars drove up to the cabin, Smokey's jaw dropped. When Smokey saw Hugh in the backseat of one squad car, he kicked the table. This was all Amy's fault! She had taken the gun, and she had stolen his car. She must have driven it to that store, and called the cops. He should have shot her when he had the chance.

Amy talked most of the way home, answering Detective Rockport's questions. Kendra fell asleep.

When their car pulled into the Edgertons' driveway, Amy woke Kendra and said, "We're home." No two words had ever sounded so good to her.

Mrs. Nordlund and the Edgertons spilled out the door before the car came to a stop. Jorja was there, too, and Amy's grandparents, and Amy's neighbor Mr. Prendell, and Mrs. Edgerton's mother, with a cast on her leg.

Television cameras lined the Edgertons' front path, waiting to capture the happy reunion. Dozens of reporters cheered spontaneously when Amy and Kendra got out of the car.

"Tubby home!" Kendra cried.

Even Detective Rockport had to wipe tears from his eyes when Amy and Kendra ran forward, and hugged their parents.

DAY SIX

Chapter Twenty-two

Darielle and Jeff waited in the Honolulu airport for their flight to be called. A TV monitor overhead was tuned to the day's headlines on CNN.

While Darielle went to the ladies' room, Jeff watched footage of the joyous reunion between Kendra Edgerton and her parents. Also present were the babysitter, Amy Nordlund, who had been kidnapped, too, and Amy's mother.

The reporter told an amazing story of how the girl had sneaked clues into DVDs that her captors had made for the Edgertons. "She let them know what kind of vehicle the kidnappers drove," the reporter said. "She told them that Kendra's nanny was involved in the plot, and gave hints that let police figure out the approximate area where Amy and Kendra were being held, all without the kidnappers catching on to what she was doing."

A girl named Jorja was interviewed, too, a friend of Amy's who had figured out the signal Amy used before she gave the clues, and who alerted the police.

When the reporter told Amy, "You are certainly lucky to be rescued," Jorja said, "It wasn't luck. Amy got rescued because she used her brain."

Jeff laughed at that, but then the photo of Darielle and Kendra by the pool flashed on the screen. "Kendra's nanny, Darielle Monroe, is still wanted for questioning. Darielle was romantically involved with one of the kidnappers and, according to public records, the cabin where the kidnappers took the girls was owned by Darielle's elderly uncle, who suffers from dementia. Anyone with information about Darielle Monroe is urged to call the police."

Jeff froze. Darielle was the girl's nanny, not a friend of the mother who was helping out, as she had said. How could she still be wanted for questioning when she had already called the police? Or had she only pretended to call?

Jeff felt sick to his stomach. He knew in his bones that Darielle was somehow responsible for the kidnapping of Kendra Edgerton.

He had intended to ask Darielle to marry him. Instead he walked to the ticket counter and said, "I need to call airport security."

Jeff pretended to sleep during most of the flight, to avoid talking to Darielle, but he kept slipping his hand into his pocket to finger the diamond ring that he had planned to give her that night. What a close call, Jeff thought. What a terrible mistake I almost made.

When Darielle stepped off the plane in Seattle, two police detectives stood at the gate, waiting for her.

Jane Delane stared at the morning newspaper. "Land's sake, Freida, would you look at this?" She pointed to the front page. "Those girls we saw at Walt's cabin were the ones who got kidnapped!"

"You're kidding!"

Freida leaned over her sister's shoulder as they both read the story.

"It mentions Leeann," Jane said. "She's credited with telling the police that there were children at the cabin."

"But we're the ones who saw those girls," Freida said. "We told Leeann! We should have our names in the paper."

"We didn't call the police," Jane said. "Leeann did."

"Well, doesn't that beat all," said Freida.

Mikey Martin's parents saw the same news story.

"I don't believe it!" Mikey's dad said. "The nanny that the police were looking for was in Honolulu when we were. That woman Mikey saw on the beach was really her!"

"No way!" said Mikey's mother.

They both stared at the blurred image of Darielle's face, looking from the backseat of a police car.

"The guy she was with saw her picture on the news and turned her in."

Mr. Martin laid the newspaper on the table and stared at his wife. "There was a twenty-thousand dollar reward for information leading to the safe return of the two girls. We could have collected it."

Mikey said, "I found two quarters under the newspaper box."

Mr. and Mrs. Edgerton asked Amy, her mother, and her grandparents to come for lunch on Saturday, to celebrate. When they arrived, Kendra, wearing a pink sunsuit, wrapped her arms around Amy's legs and said, "Tubby love Amy."

When they had eaten, Mrs. Edgerton turned to Amy. "Would you consider being our regular babysitter this summer?" she asked. "I'm taking next week off and then I'll only work afternoons. We'd need you from one until six, five days a week." She named a weekly amount that was far more than Amy had expected.

"I'd love to be Kendra's sitter," Amy said.

"Then it's settled," Mr. Edgerton said.

Mrs. Nordlund beamed at Amy. "I'm so proud of you," she said. "Your dad would be proud of you, too."

Yes, Amy thought. This time, Dad would be proud of me.

Kendra said, "Tubby play game."

"All right," Amy said. "What would you and Tubby like to play?"

Kendra began running laps around the family room. "Mama donkey say heehaw," she shouted. "Tubby say heehaw! Heehaw!"